"What a fun read! These were turbulent times, and Philip Mallory's collection of letters is a chronicle of adventure and a glimpse into the heart and soul of this sensitive young man. His French schooling, rowdy fellow students, and the ever-looming mountain are the rungs on his ladder of personal growth."

- John Howard, U.S. Olympic Cyclist
  Pan American Games Cycling Champion
  Hawaii Ironman Triathlon Champion
  Bicycle Land Speed Record Holder

MORE THAN A
MOUNTAIN

My Year Cycling in France

by
Philip R. Mallory II

More Than a Mountain
My Year Cycling in France

ISBN: 0-9745842-0-7

First Printing, October, 2003

World Cycling Press
3910 Chapman Street
San Diego, CA 92110-5694
USA
619-224-1050
philipmallory1@hotmail.com

This book is dedicated to every generation,
even those to come,
but especially to my family.

Introduction

This is what it is. You may call it a short book. You may call it a long poem. You might even call it demented, psychotic ramblings from an inane loser whose only asset is that he has guts enough to write an autobiography before he even gets to college.

But what it will always be is a story, no matter what. My story. A story that I hope you'll enjoy. But also, for those who might be my age or close, a book that you might learn something from.

I am an eighteen-year-old student at Torrey Pines High School in San Diego, and last year I changed my life by deciding to be an exchange student in France. I was trying to escape the dead-end I saw in my life as it was.

I had a great time in France, and I now feel compelled to tell the story of this adventurous year I spent so far from home, where I learned that taking risks and climbing mountains could help me grow and change in ways that will stay with me forever.

The book that you are now reading evolved from a series of weekly letters that were written less than weekly, but the effort has to count for something, right? After I got back home I looked at my letters again, and it refreshed my memory, but I realized that my memory wouldn't always work that well, and I needed to write the whole story down before it slipped away.

Anyway, the letters are still in there, sometimes a little more elaborate than when they were sent, sometimes with insight added afterwards. For better or worse, this is how I have decided to tell my story.

For those of you who do not know me personally I must warn you that I joke around frequently, and I like to do it. But it is

1

for you that I'm writing this book. If you could come visit me we could talk about all this, and you wouldn't have to scan your eyes over lines of weird shapes we like to call letters to read what I have to say.

So bear with me. Know that I joke around, but I intend to get a story across, with perhaps a couple of lessons along the way.

Also, I go from subject to subject in a lot of these letters because I found that I had something to say and the opportunity to say it. I did not change the order or randomness of the letters because I thought that they might lose something valuable in the process.

And finally, I would like to add this: after being removed from my culture I became much more able to look at things from an outsider's point of view. I've basically learned to be more open minded about everything from politics to culture to what we've been brought up to believe.

I hope that I can open your eyes, too.

Philip Mallory, August 15, 2003

Chapter 1
Getting There

October 15, 2001

Dear All,

I'm sorry if I've been silent. I'll tell you what's been going on. Warning, this is going to take a while. Get comfortable.

Leaving America:

The French consulate is nothing if not French. On September 25, 2001, the day before I was scheduled to leave and after having corresponded and phoned and negotiated for months, Dad and I still didn't know whether or not we were going to get my visa. It was scary.

On the very last day, full of fear and hope, we drove up from our home north of San Diego to the consulate in Los Angeles. Then, after all our worrying, we got the visa in 15 minutes flat. Typical.

Since it was ten o'clock in the morning, and I wasn't scheduled to fly out until ten that night, we wondered what to do with the rest of the day.

It would be a waste of time to go all the way back home to San Diego for a couple of hours. We considered going to the movies but finally decided on Disneyland. Cool, Right?

Dad and I quickly got lost on the way there, and then just as quickly we re-found ourselves. Disneyland, here we come!

We had a blast! It was awesome. I got to do some things that I had never done because the lines had always been too long. And since this was a weekday and only a couple of weeks after September 11th, there were about 17 people in the whole park.

No waits were longer than five minutes. It must have been over 100 degrees that day so, needless to say, at the end of the day we were both tired. We did everything we wanted to and then left.

My flight was scheduled to leave from Long Beach at ten PM. We got there nice and early, watched my luggage get unpacked, searched and then repacked again. We sat around, wasted time people-watching, and also talked a little.

Neither of us really knew what to say or do. It was awkward in that we both knew and accepted that I was leaving, that it would be good for me, and that when I came back I would be a better, wiser person. Or at least different.

When it was finally my time, Dad shook my hand and said, "Do good."

And I went in, a little teary I might add, and sat down in one of those airport seats that are annoyingly connected to the ones next to them. I sat in that uncomfortable airport seat and waited for them to call my airplane seat, probably more uncomfortable than the one I was already in.

I waited for somebody to look at me and ask why I was crying. I decided to simply reply, "I'm an exchange student," and leave it at that.

That person never looked, never asked. I did get into a conversation on the plane to New York, but I said to myself that it wasn't really going to add up to anything. I felt that it just wouldn't change much and that it was useless for me to participate in it. I was leaving.

Five hours later I was in New York

I felt alone … not that I was lonely, but from then on I knew that I would have to do things on my own and watch out for myself. I had to become independent and provide for myself. I'm sure people expect this feeling when they're going away to college, but I was dealing with it much earlier than they, but I wasn't worried at all. I thought I would be provided for wherever I went.

Life, unfortunately, isn't so dreamy.

In New York I was the first person from AFS (The American Field Service Student Exchange Program) to arrive. I got my baggage, and an AFS volunteer spotted me. She told me to wait where I was and see if I could find others while she went off on her own quest to find poor unlucky AFSers.

So I put on my music, and I quietly waited around. Then I saw another guy with an AFS badge and waved him over. One down. It wasn't too hard to spot them; there weren't many people in the airport.

Two hours later I arrived at the hotel with three girls and the other guy. Of thirteen people from AFS who were meeting at the hotel for orientation, only two were guys, including me. That was only a taste of what was to come as far as being outnumbered sex-wise.

The orientation was pretty fun overall; the food at the hotel was crap, though. You could drop five bucks on a huge piece of chocolate cake and then half way through look down at it and say, "I don't want any more of this."

I tried to adjust a little to the time change, but it was pretty difficult.

The following day we got on our plane to Brussels, Belgium.

Arriving in Europe:

We got to Belgium after a pretty normal trans-Atlantic flight. I didn't sleep a wink, even though it was an over-nighter. I don't do that.

We had to transfer to our flight to Paris without the aid of an AFS representative. After two hours we found that there was a pilot strike. No flights. We were faced with a dilemma.

For the first time in our AFS experience one of us had to take charge because there was nobody else there to give a hoot about thirteen Americans. After three years of high school French and two weeks skiing at Val d'Isere last year, I could speak French a little better than the others, so I found myself in charge of struggling to look for a solution with the airline in my broken French and sometimes English. Finally, I got the plane tickets changed into train tickets (1st class, baby!).

I got a lady from Sabena Airlines to let me use the phone to call AFS France. They understood and said to arrive as quickly as possible. Problem was that Sabena still had our luggage, and after several hours it still hadn't come out.

Everybody migrated to the baggage claim. People slept clutching their carry-on baggage so that it wouldn't be stolen. I played solitaire, as I was the only one awake, and carefully kept one eye on the baggage carrousel.

I heard myself say, almost to myself, "Hey, that's my baggage!" and everybody jumped up as if they weren't sleeping after all. It was frightening. We had waited much too long.

We walked a ways to the train station. We got on a connecting train, and for the first time we caught a glimpse of Europe and what would be in store for us in the coming nine months. I said, "You see them trees? Them be Belgian trees."

It was the first glimpse of Europe not on a post card for the other twelve AFSers.

We got to our high-speed train, or *train grande vitesse* in French. It was really cool. We were burning up the countryside. Everybody slept. I got pictures of people sleeping. I don't sleep on trips like that, even though I was exhausted and smelly from lugging around everyone else's luggage that all weighed 50 to 60 pounds. They were all girls, and girls pack a ton of luggage. There's no more discussion about it.

We arrived at the Charles de Gaulle train station northeast of Paris. We started for the point where we were supposed to meet an AFS volunteer, but we were stopped by big army guys in cammies carrying big guns. There had been a bag left unattended in the station, and they thought it might be a bomb.

They moved us 300 meters away … because that would protect us from a big explosion. Trouble was the bomb was between the meeting point and us.

Two hours later the guy who left the bag came back, said it wasn't a bomb, and everybody went home happy, kind of.

After two more hours in a bus sitting in traffic I hit the sack at our youth hostel outside Paris. I hadn't slept in 42 hours.

The next day we toured Paris, but I don't remember much. I was wasted. At least my pictures will be interesting, if nothing else.

After some orientation and two nights sleep, I got on a bus at 5:30 in the morning. We were on the way to the *Gare de Lyon* (one of the many Parisian train stations).

On the way I saw a nun, yes a nun, yelling at this nice looking couple for taking her parking spot while three prostitutes walked by.

"What the hell have I done to myself?" I asked, burying my head in my hands. Holy S§~t. *Trente-six fois merde!*

(My Dad has told me *"trente-six fois merde"* was one of my grandfather's favorite expressions. He was born in the States but had spent most of his first thirteen years in France, and he had spoken French before English. I'm sort of following in his footsteps, although unintentionally.

I don't think I'll translate *"trente-six fois merde"* for you.)

The *Gare de Lyon* before dawn. My *TGV* is on the right.

***

Arriving in *Le Teil*:

I caught the southbound *TGV* and watched the countryside fly by. During that trip I did not once see the sun.

I arrived in *Valence*, a nice city in the *Rhône* Valley south of *Lyon*, and was met by my host-Dad and sister, with her boyfriend along for the ride.

I am quickly submerged in the phenomenon of *la bise.* That's the kissing-on-the-cheek thing. Three times here, but it varies by region.

Whoa! And with the guys, you have to make a special effort to shake everybody's hand. That was a scary thing for an American. People don't like to touch each other so much in the U.S., but here I was meeting people for the first time and kissing them already.

If only this system worked with the girls back home. Now that would be cool. I'd be willing to be a trendsetter.

My host-family is great, but it will have to be short-lived, since I can only stay for two months. They are moving into a smaller house, so I will have to move on.

When I talked about the situation of boarding with eleven girls and one guy and said that that was only a taste of what was to come, I wasn't joking. Here I am living with three women, two dogs (girls) and one cat (girl.) And the dad is a salesman and only at home for the weekends.

He has the habit of saying, "Oh, eat this. It's a specialty of the region." So far he has said that about fifteen times. Apparently, there are a lot of regional specialties. Lots of cheese and wine here, and I am learning a lot.

The food is good, but not great. I'm sure I'll get used to it.

School is good here. The math, science, and that type of stuff are easy, but in my French class we're reading *Victor Hugo.* My history class is hard because the lady is crazy, and I can't understand her. I'm also in English 1. It's actually the fourth year of study, but they don't actually speak at all.

I've spoken to other Americans here, and they concur. French kids study it, but they can't speak English. It's not like all Americans can speak French, but the French are surrounded by the English language, while Americans are surrounded only by themselves.

In school I've learned a lot (of bad words), and I find that I think in French most of the time, and my English is deteriorating. This letter has been a real task to write, and I've erased most of it because I say, "That doesn't work," or "That just sounds stupid." You guys are lucky that I'm so cool and that I'm committed to writing all this crap down.

***

I've done a lot of cycling here. It's been so cool cycling in the country that's the most famous for it. Back in the States for several years before embarking on "my journey," I had been racing my bike on the road and on the track. Now I have come to Mecca.

I've bought a beautiful French bike, and I'm going to climb *le Mont Ventoux*, a mysterious mountain famous with cyclists. I've dreamed about this barren pile of rocks even in San Diego. I've dreamed about this bump on the map because all my life I have studied the legendary figures of the *Tour de France*, men who have had to suffer up this mountain.

Now I wanted to make my own history, instead of learning about somebody else's.

People tell me I'm a good climber on the bike, but I have a suspicion that I haven't seen anything yet. The weather here is kind of dodgy. I'm including here an excerpt from my cycling journal to give you an idea:

"Today was a mess. I rode for about an hour and half on a course that if I try, can take me about 35 minutes round trip.

"The wind was gusting at 120 kph. It really wasn't so bad on the street or when I left from my house, with lots of trees and big houses around. But alleyways post a huge problem. You're going with strong wind, sure, but all of a sudden from the left or right the wind is coming at 60 kph. I weigh about three kilos, so I'm just like the leaves in the wind.

"Which posed another big problem. The leaves got in my eyes, and I couldn't see. And crossing the *Rhône* River. Jesus Christ. There is no protection and the wind just fires down the valley. I crossed on foot, desperately gripping onto the guardrail and my bike. My bike was practically horizontal; I don't think it once touched the ground going across that bridge. I fell two or three times when I was actually riding, but I was going like 2 kph. It might not have been the best idea to go out today, but I had to go to the bike shop.

"I've bought all my winter clothes and finalized all the stuff on my *Look* bicycle.

Look is a famous bicycle brand in *France*. It's a beautiful yellow and has a very high-tech looking aluminum frame with a sloping top tube to minimize the size of the rear triangle, which is supposed to do cool, important things. It has three chain rings in the front and a nine-speed cassette in back.

The owner of the local bike shop here says he will paint my name on the bike, just like the pros do. I'll bring it back to the States after my year in France is over.

I'm going to the bike shop to pick it up on Wednesday and then hopefully catch that Wednesday ride because I've made friends and then kind of disappeared without saying goodbye when my brake cable broke last week.

I also wanted to measure myself up to the riders here since I haven't come across any.

"My winter clothes are just like the rubber "death suit" that my Dad used to use to make lightweight when he was rowing. My tights are like an inch thick. It's crazy, but I'll sure be glad not to be a human popsicle. In my really heavy jacket there is a baklava. Snow is cold. I'll be the most prepared in San Diego if a freak blizzard hits. I am switching Sunday and Saturday training. It's supposed to be better tomorrow."

***

Sorry about the language. It was one heck of day. This excerpt is from the next day and I've added nothing:

"It was the calmest day today. It was even kind of creepy. No wind at all anywhere. The storm blew itself out, I guess.

"At like 2:30 this morning thunder and lighting were all around our house. Man, thunder and lightning are really cool when they're far away and you can look at it while the sky lights up, but not when it's right next to you. Scary.

"Anyway, 14 kilometers of climbing today. I went to the top of the only big mountain I know how to get to. It took me around 55 minutes. During that time I did two 20-minute pieces and cruised the rest of the time.

"Sometimes I would get out of the saddle and would start flying, not knowing why or feeling anything, and other times nothing. That happened three or four times. Maybe that's what it's like to be good. All in all, I did three pieces of 20 minutes. I think I could do the mountain in 45 minutes. Maybe that should be a goal before *le Mont Ventoux*.

"It was unbelievably beautiful here today after all the rain during the night. There were waterfalls all around, and everything was especially green. The sheep and the cows were playing around; it was just really cool. I've never been this excited to just go ride. I think this is the happiest I've ever been. Now all I have to do is learn this stupid language.

"I'm not homesick at all. I miss my Dad, but I miss just being with him and joking around, and I would kill for a Domino's pizza.

"Other than that, I'm great."

And that's that. I was so excited to ride, since it was so peaceful, and I was so happy because all this riding made me feel invincible.

I'm planning on doing *le Ventoux* on Halloween. That'll be good.

I love you all and will try to get back to you on a regular basis from now on. Don't hesitate to write back.

Philip Mallory

***

I wrote this letter to catch up with everybody. I didn't know before I left that I would be writing letters to everybody, so this is the first in a series to follow. Little did I know that I was not invincible after all.

Chapter 2
Disaster Strikes

October 20, 2001

Le Mont Ventoux, one of the most historic climbs in *France*. The bald mountain looming over *Provence*. Twenty-three kilometers long, and I've wanted to climb it ever since I knew of its existence. And now I was living only 100 kilometers north of it. On a clear day I thought I could see it.

Photo credit: www.lemontventoux.net
The treeless summit of *le Mont Ventoux*

I figured I could ride there with the wind blowing in my direction and then climb the beast. Then I hoped I could get a ride home from somebody. I planned it all out. I bought a map. I knew every road I had to take to get there. I trained for it. I rode up hills that I never would have imagined doing otherwise. I trained during lunch break at school. I bought a new bike. All in all, I was ready. I bought the warmest cycling clothes I could find, as it was getting late in the season to be riding up to elevation. I was ready. Halloween was the date.

I really believed I could do it. I was convinced that I was good enough. I was convinced I was going to succeed. No mountain had ever beaten me before. I had worked until I was cross-eyed just to get the opportunity.

I never got the opportunity that I had worked so hard for.

You see *le Ventoux* acts as the border between the *Drôme* and *Vaucluse* regions of France. I could ride my bike in the *Drôme* region but not in the *Vaucluse*. AFS said "no way." I would have to fill out a ton of forms and have my Dad sign something, and then I'd only be allowed to go with a group.

I basically thought that was bullshit, and I made sure that people knew my feelings. I was pissed, to say the least. I couldn't do what I wanted. For the first time I realized that my life in France was not as free as it used to be in the United States, or rather how privileged my life in the U.S. actually was. I felt threatened by all the restrictions. There are always restrictions, no matter how high you get, and most are for your own well-being, but some seem to have no reason and all you want to do is get around them. I felt like I was being treated like a ten-year-old. I understood why people would be concerned. I know it's dangerous to ride your bike, especially 100 kilometers from home, but I felt somehow that it still wasn't fair. I felt cheated.

Everything is dangerous. Going outside in the morning is dangerous. But somehow you've got to get up. Life isn't worth living if you try to rule out all danger.

I once read in a book that you could never be free until you realized that you were already dead. I certainly don't want to die, and I'm not going to do anything stupid to try to buy myself an early grave, but I'm going to live my life for what it's worth. Does that make me a daredevil? I don't think so, but everyone has his or her opinion.

Chapter 3
Getting There #2

3 novembre 2001

Dear All,

I hope you are all doing well. I have moved here in *France*, and I was not too happy about it, at least initially.

There was a telephone call. We were eating dinner around 8:30 on a Thursday night. My host-Mom got up and answered. She talked, and I kept with the conservation I was having with my host-sister. My host-Mom returned, started eating and then told me that the phone call was AFS and that I was moving to *Tournon*, around 100 kilometers up the *Rhône* River north of *Le Teil*, the next day, and I had to be there at 15:00. (That's 3 PM.)

My jaw dropped. I was pissed. Just that day I was talking to a nice local cycling family and it looked like I could stay with them, and then I get some random phone call where the person didn't even ask to talk to me directly to give me (in my mind) terrible news.

I thought I had three to four weeks to find a family and set it all up before I had to move. What's going on? I was not at all happy with the less than 24 hours notice, the fact that I was moving to a completely different town, and that the person didn't even want to talk to me.

Not happy at all.

Over the phone from the States my Dad told me that it might not be all that bad, that maybe things would be great up there, and I might be a ton happier than I would be in *Le Teil*. But I didn't even know about the opportunities I might discover in *Le Teil*, so I wasn't happy giving them up to find something new.

But after further thought, I realized that if I had done well in *Le Teil* I could certainly do well in *Tournon*. All I needed was confidence.

***

Tournon is not bad so far. It's a beautiful little town with a majestic *chateau* as a centerpiece. Confidence has helped.

There's lots of cycling, and even a rowing club. (My Dad and Granddad and even Great-Grandfather had been rowers, and I had been a California champion in rowing.)

And my school, the *Lycée Gabriel-Faure*, was built in 1536 and is the oldest *lycée* in *France*. There is one particular hall lined with old tapestries where you just want to hit the suckers and watch at least 200 years of dust fall off. The tapestries are pre-Renaissance and early Renaissance and must have been much more beautiful back then. They've had a rough life, I'm sure.

I've studied stuff this old and now I can actually see these things in their natural setting that have been looked upon by generation after generation, story after story, history after history.

I felt I was in a place full of importance even though I was in a dark hallway off the beaten path.

***

There are two bridges across the *Rhône* in *Tournon*. The older one is one of the first suspension bridges ever built anywhere in the World. It is now a pedestrian bridge.

Here is *Tournon* on the near side of the *Rhône* River. The historic bridge is the closer of the two, and you can see the *chateau* just below the bridge.

This whole region produces the deep rich red *Côtes du Rhône* wines *(côtes* means hillsides). *Le vin d'appelation St. Joseph* is produced in *Tournon.* On the other side of the river is *Tain l'Hermitage*, also famous for its wines. At the top of the hill behind *Tain* is a small chapel to bless the vineyards.

Vineyards on the hill behind *Tain.* The chapel is at the top.

The chapel

***

I assumed my new host-parents were really old. I told my American Dad so on the phone. They look it, believe me. But they are both 58. And since my real Dad is 57, he wasn't too happy to find out that they look so old to me.

Dad looks young for his age, though.

My host-parents smoke, which could explain the looking old thing, but they've produced beautiful children. The youngest is now working as a travel agent in San Francisco, and we have spoken via WebCam in English, or American as everyone here likes to say.

I will admit she speaks better English than I speak French, but she's got seven years on me, and I know and hope that I will learn a lot.

My host-parents are very funny, but my host-Mom knows way too many people. In *France* it's not polite if you know someone you haven't seen for a week and not stop and ask how the kids are and all that, so it takes forever to just walk down the street. And since they've been here for the last 22 years, they actually do know everybody.

And that's about that.

À la prochaine,

Philippe

***

My host-parents are great people. I have come to learn that there are good, caring people everywhere, in every state, in every country, but few can match my new host-parents.

My host-Mom's name is *Liliane,* which I eventually changed to *Maman Lou-Lou.* My host-Dad's name is *Jean-Claude,* whom I jokingly refer to as *Jesus (JC.)*

***

This is a story I like to tell and an anecdote that people seem to like. Since my voyage came right after September 11th there was a lot of concern everywhere about everything. So here goes.

September 11th seemed to be a special day in world history. Although not for everybody, this day was a day of great sorrow for me and most of those in the United States. It was a little under two weeks before I left. I got up at six o'clock and turned on the radio.

Apparently there had been a huge accident and a plane had flown into one of the World Trade Center buildings.

Then another.

I turned on the TV to find a huge, national disaster. I went to school. I saw girls crying. I ditched and went home. I turned on the TV. I saw myself crying.

I was looking for answers. Things seemed to happen so fast. People had died, and America was demoted to watching television and holding on to loved ones, knowing that not every New Yorker would have that privilege. Flags were put up. On cars. In windows. Things stopped.

I became scared that things would happen again. The first night I was in *Tournon* I went to walk the dog. It was night. I heard this loud rumbling. I thought it could be something like a nuclear explosion at *Paris* or *Lyon*. I looked at my watch and said to myself that I would be able to say I heard it if it really happened.

Turned out it was a train going over a bridge, but it shows how scared I was. I was looking for somebody to save 2001 but scared that somebody was going to ruin it beyond recognition.

***

I had to fit this in here somewhere so here goes....

I need to explain the *Ardèche* and *Drôme* regions. *Regions* are kind of like states in the U.S., except they are smaller, since *France* is a smaller country.

I was living in the *Ardèche* region, but across the *Rhône* River is the *Drôme*. There was lots of riding in both regions, but the *Ardèche* is much more mountainous.

Not mountains like *les Alps*, with jagged peaks above the tree line. Mountains with farms and villages and forests and lakes.

Both the *Drôme* and the *Ardèche* are very pretty, but I do think that the *Ardèche* is prettier. The mountains rise behind my house in *Tournon,* and there are beautiful roads through steep gorges thick with trees on both sides, and when you go through the forest, the temperature drops a couple notches.

Photo credit: Christian Nicollet

It's great fun after living in San Diego all my life. Spring is so much prettier in the *Ardèche.* There is more livestock farming rather than crops and other "boring" things to grow. It's cooler to be zooming along on your bike and look at cows and goats rather than corn.

There is a big rivalry between the *Drôme* and the *Ardèche*. The wine, the cycling, the tourists, are all involved in this rivalry.

There are bigger cities in the *Drôme*. *Valence* and *Montélimar* are the biggest. Look again at the picture on page 19. *Tain L'Hermitage* is the city that is directly across the river from *Tournon*. They could be one city, but they aren't, and you don't really ask why. The trains pass on the *Drôme* side of the river, but the largest bike race in all of *Europe* is in the *Ardèche*.

It's a bit "tit for tat." Petty stuff, really.

I love the *Drôme*, but the *Ardèche* will always be my home away from home.

Chapter 4
What's Between Fall and Spring?

13 novembre 2001

Dear All,

I hope you are well. I certainly am.

Living in San Diego is living in a very structured and boring climate. Nothing changes. It's always "nice."

So now the first real winter of my life has arrived, with the grass freezing every night and the temperature only around 3° C every day. There is a huge wind here, often over 100 kph. It is called *Le Mistral*.

I've talked about it before, but I didn't know it had a name. It just whips down the *Rhône* Valley to the Mediterranean.

It's completely dark here at 5:30 PM, and I found myself a little depressed for a while without the sun. It's the worst on Tuesday because I have school from 8:00 to 5:30. It's cold outside and the air is dense with cigarette smoke, so the other non-smokers and I take to the hallways. I never really get to see the sun, but the other days I get out at noon and can see almost all the sun I need.

There is something really ironic here. This is *Tournon*, a small town by almost anyone's terms. I take physical education here with the Junior/Senior people. It's a two-hour class, and before and after you can see everybody smoking cigarettes. Whoa! Kind of defeats the purpose of PE, doesn't it?

In PE we're playing badminton. I always saw it as a nice friendly game to be played in the sunshine by royalty and pretty women. Not here. It's savage here. Even the girls hit that little ball-thing like it deserves to die. Cultural differences, I guess.

***

With the winter arriving, everyone is talking about snow and skiing. I am going to scout out *l'Alpe d'Huez* with the *Tournon* ski club before Dad comes over at Christmas and we go skiing there together. I was kind of uneasy about going without Dad because the road to the ski village is such a famous cycling climb that I wanted to share the first time with him.

This is just another thing I'm going to have to do by myself.

***

My host-parents' oldest daughter was robbed. No more computer, TV, car, all that. To make her feel better I made fajitas with a very limited supply of available Mexican food. Just as an example, I bought Thai rice, mixed in the salsa ketchup stuff I found with some hot sauce to make Mexican rice. It was too sticky, though.

I spent around six hours cooking off-and-on. It was really good. I did everything, much to the dismay of my host-Dad. He said that he was sure he would like it, but he was going to get good and liquored up first.

He is a very funny guy, and he and his wife are growing on me all the time.

Meanwhile I'm understanding more and more, and making strides in my pronunciation. *Lou-Lou*, my host-Mom, has really been working hard with me. She grinds me because she really knows how much I want to speak French well, and she cares about me too much to let me slack off.

Love,

Philippe Malloire

26

***

Pierre Malloire is a name that my Dad, born Peter Mallory, made up when he was in prep-school. It was an all boys' school, so it must have been pretty boring. In addition to being boring it must have sucked. In his boredom Dad invented this name because in a good French accent it sounds very evil and very French. I took up this name, and most people now call me "Malloire." It seems to fit.

***

I'll take this opportunity to talk about JC and Lou-Lou.

My host parents and me

JC and Lou-Lou care. They really do. They become frustrated when I screw up, and when they come down on me it's like a ton of bricks. But they are genuinely interested in teaching me as much as possible and making sure that I have only nice things to "report" to the American population. I guess that's what I'm doing now.

I don't know if I know anybody better than I know them, and I only have nice things to say about them. I don't have the same liberty that I had with my Dad, but I don't need it, now that I think about it. They are really giving people, and I deeply appreciate everything they do for me.

Chapter 5
Where'd All the Turkeys Go?

23 novembre 2001

Dear All,

Happy Turkey Day. I'm a little late, I know, but you all are probably still full the day after, and as for me, I'm hungry. I hope you'll enjoy the leftovers. Here, my family knew that Thanksgiving is very special, so I got to pop my first bottle of *champagne*. It was pretty good, but I still like guzzling the Sparkling Apple Cider, which defines a traditional Thanksgiving for me. It's just as bubbly, but if you try to chug champagne you'll wake up the next day with one hell of a headache.

I've had to explain everything that we eat on Thanksgiving, but these people don't know what cranberries are. C'mon!

***

School here is good. It's a little bit brighter. I took a test in English today. The assignment was to write an essay with a choice of subjects, and it had to have more than 200 words. I practically wrote a novel. We had three hours. I wrote the whole time.

I asked the teacher, who kind of speaks English, if I could choose my own topic. She said sure. I wrote about the philosophy of God, whether He exists or not, and why He would be interpreted differently in different cultures.

I calculated (I didn't say counted) that I wrote over 2,000 words. It was pretty funny. Lots of people were nowhere near 200 words. I guess I like to write, and you're reading some of the proof of that.

Besides, talking about God is a very controversial topic, so it's more fun to read and write about.

Today it snowed at 300 meters elevation. I just hope there is snow when I go skiing December 2nd at *l'Alpe d'Huez* with the ski club. *Les Alps* aren't far from here, so skiing is huge.

Apparently, it's not going to snow too much here in town. It is pretty darn cold already though. I was riding my bike with a group last Sunday. It was the morning, so it was maybe 2° Celsius (35° Fahrenheit) and kind of raining. After the top of the mountain I took a drink of water, put some more clothes on for the descent and ate a little something, all while descending at 50 kph and taking hairpin turns like nothing.

By the bottom I noticed that my lips had frozen together.

I breathe through my nose on the descents and stay still so I can feel my heartbeat and I count. I try to get my heart under 80 beats per minute for a little bit. It's hard because I do a lot of work and because I don't know the descents very well, which means that the adrenaline is always rushing.

I'm going to go visit *le Mont Ventoux* this Sunday. I am still blindingly mad that I couldn't climb it last month. I inquired, and it was closed due to snow about a week ago.

Il fait froid!

I love you all.

Happy Thanksgiving,

Malloire

Chapter 6
Le Ventoux from a Distance

28 novembre 2001

Dear All,

Another weekly report from the kid in *France*.

I was sick on Sunday and Monday. On Saturday I did 95 kilometers on my bike, and breathing in the cold air made me sick. It was barely above freezing.

On Monday I went to the doctor, and he said that there are just a ton of diseases that I haven't seen because it's winter here, and these diseases can't exist in San Diego because of the difference in climate.

I was sick, but that did not stop me from going *to le Mont Ventoux* with my host-family. It was blocked off at 1,500 m but I still enjoyed seeing it and seeing the top, if only from a distance. I can't wait until I can climb it on my bike. All 23 kilometers of it going up to 1,909m elevation. (That's over 6,000 feet!)

In some ways I'm glad it's winter. I'll go skiing this weekend in *les Alps*, and I've never really had a winter, but I'm also waiting for the spring when I can really get the kilometers on my bike.

There is a big race/ride in my region. It's called the *Ardéchoise*. It's absolutely huge here, and I will be barely old enough to do it next June.

There were almost 11,000 people who participated last year. I'll have a priority number because I am recognized here as a strong rider. That means I won't have to wade through the oceans of people on bikes, many of whom I'm sure will not be going very quickly.

I'm really excited about doing it.

***

I went to a grown-up party the other day. A sleeper, right? It would have been if it were in San Diego.

Since I am an American, people are interested in getting to know me, which feels great. People actually want to meet me! I had a great time talking to everybody. A guy even said that my French was almost without an accent. The lady right next to him shook her head, but hey, that's still pretty good. I'll accept whatever comes.

It was great. Here I am drinking wine and eating cheese, almost like the French. When I come back, I'll be the one to call to tell you what's good and what's just decent.

***

It's a huge wine region here. It looks a little sad now because the hills are covered in vines which are brown and dead instead of green and lively. It'll look cool when it starts to snow, but that's still a little ways off, if it does indeed snow.

I have concluded the weekly report from me in *France*.

Thanks for reading.

Malloire

***

I went to *l'Alpe d'Huez* with the ski club on the second of December. It was an amazing experience.

Lance Armstrong had dominated on that climb less than six months before in the 2001 *Tour de France*. I could still see the painting on the road that encouraged all the riders. As I sat at the front of the bus I marveled at it all. "Go Lance." "*Virenque.*" "*Telekom.*" I had watched it all sitting on the floor in front of my television 9,000 kilometers away. And now I was there.

I guess it's like any sporting event. You don't really know until you're right there seeing with your own eyes, not through the television, how much something can mean to you.

I had a terrible day of skiing since there was more water than snow on *les Alps* but I wouldn't give up that day for anything. It was truly special.

L'Alpe d'Huez on *2 decembre 2001.*

***

21 decembre 2001

Dad and I have been missing each other, as every exchange student misses his parents. Dad decided to come over and visit me over the holidays and take me to do some sightseeing that I hadn't had the chance to do.

We made plans, and when he finally arrived I was taking a nap.

You see, I have figured something out. Time passes. It never speeds up or slows down. It may seem to, but it really doesn't.

I think about this kind of stuff when I'm walking down the street. I say to myself, "I'm going to get to where I am walking. I just need to walk and wait." So I figured that Dad would come over, and I would see him. I just needed to wait, and, in this case, I took a nap.

Sleeping is an easy way to have time pass away. Before, when my life wasn't going where I wanted it to and I was depressed, I would just sleep all the time, to get out of having to deal with stuff, instead of taking action and actually changing my life for the better.

I just put off my problems, which doesn't help at all.

Don't do that!

So time passed, Dad came, and then before I knew it vacation was over. But not before doing a whole lot.

Chapter 7
Vacation is All I Ever Wanted

9 janvier 2002

Dear All,

     I hope you are all doing well. I just got back from vacation with my Dad over Christmas break. It was exhausting. Dad and I covered a ton of ground.

     Thanks to *Air France*, he had arrived without his baggage. That always sucks. We spent hours on the phone with airline people, so we could get all that damn stuff back. He had ski stuff, presents, not to mention his clothes. Two days later the airline dropped off his baggage around midnight.

     So we went skiing at *l'Alpe d'Huez*, as we had planned.

L'Alpe d'Huez on *26 decembre 2001.*

I showed the climb to Dad as we drove up after dark. Right then and there Dad promised to return next summer so we could climb it together.

I decided not to mention to him that we could also do *le Mont Ventoux* next summer.

There wasn't much snow when we got there, which was reminiscent of the time I had been there three weeks earlier, but it snowed during our stay.

We found some really fun runs, but they were far out of the way.

Dad wasn't as strong as I was after my spending hundreds of kilometers racing up mountains on my bike. We didn't ski all that much, but we would get back to our hotel in the mid afternoon and take a nap or watch *Eurosport* (like ESPN). We watched the ski jumping competitions and other ski stuff.

We talked a lot, and I never remember laughing so much in my life. I had forgotten what a funny guy my Dad was.

It was refreshing to see him after so long. It felt surreal. I was in *France*, where I felt I was the King of my own domain, and then Dad comes along and joins me as a friend.

We left *l'Alpe d'Huez*, but I was ready to move on. We went back home to pick up some stuff and then hopped into our rental car, which we would get to know very well over the next week.

We headed almost due east for the *Dordogne* region. We visited *la Grotte de Font-de-Gaume*, the last prehistoric cave painting site in the world still open to the public.

Cave paintings at *Font-de-Gaume*.

We took the tour, and it really didn't sink in until much later that people thousands of years ago had done all that. It was very interesting, but it was kind of depressing. What are we, as a species, going to leave behind for others to see? Are we going to destroy this planet before people of the future get the chance to look at what we left behind, like Dad and I looked at what these prehistoric men left behind?

I dunno.

We stayed the night in the gorgeously preserved medieval city of *Sarlat*, where we bought *pâté de foie gras*, one of the most delicious things you can put on a cracker. It's made from goose liver, and this town flourishes around the production and sale of this expensive delicacy.

We arrived on a Wednesday, when the entire city was shut down for the farmers' market. We got a couple things and met a couple of very nice Americans in a pizza place before moving on.

***

We then traveled to the *chateaux* (that's plural in French, but consists of only two in our case) of the *Loire* River. The majesty of it all impressed me, but it was kind of dry and lonely. I wouldn't want to live there.

Chateau de Chambord

The *Chateau de Chambord* is the one I commented would be lonely to live in. Supposedly it was designed by Leonardo da Vinci. It has double-helix stairways, and it's enormous, with fireplaces that have turned entire walls black. The roof is amazing with all its spires, but inside it's cold, dark and depressing.

And to think that it was only a hunting lodge is just crazy. You'd have to put a thousand people in there before it would fill up.

***

We left the 16th Century behind and headed north back into the 21st Century, to city of *Le Mans* where they hold the world famous 24-hour car race. It's really cool because most of the race is held on roads open to traffic during the year.

It was so quiet the morning we were there. No Ferraris. No Porsches. It was tempting to really haul ass, but we didn't. It was really cold, and the curbs all had ice on them.

Me, the rental car and the *Mulsanne* Straight, *Le Mans*

We tried to see if we could get into the grandstand area and maybe take a tour or something, but everything was closed.

Frost on the tire barrier, Le Mans

Then it was up to *Normandie and* back to the 11th Century, where we visited the *Bayeux* Tapestry, the story of the Battle of Hastings in 1066 told on a tapestry that is 70 meters long. It was pretty amazing.

Photo Credit: www.heraldicconnections.com
William the Conqueror attacks at the Battle of Hastings

***

But here is my favorite part of the trip. Dad and I visited the Allied Invasion beaches in *Normandie*. Those beaches mean so much to so many people, and one of those people is me.

D-Day was a very special day, June 6th, 1944. All of the Allies might was shown that day, and what a day it was.

Omaha Beach 7 juin 1944

I am definitely planning on joining the military, and this was such a huge part of history. We weren't visiting a museum or anything. We were there where it happened.

Trenches, bomb craters, barbed wire is all still there.

We arrived at some pillbox gun placements overlooking the ocean. Everything was in tatters, as well it should have been. I found myself crying, just looking out to sea.

Dad didn't understand completely or something. He wanted to keep moving because it was getting late in the day and sunlight was running out. I said that I couldn't leave right then. He even got a little impatient and got in the car.

I looked out and imagined that I saw hundreds of boats and planes coming to bomb the Atlantic Wall. I could really see it.

Omaha and Utah Beaches, *31 decembre 2001, Pointe du Hoc* in the distance

It seemed to skim over Dad, and for that I have to feel kind of sorry for him. All the great things I saw in that instant, he didn't. He missed out.

When we finally did get moving we went on to *Pointe du Hoc*, the famous site where a U.S. Army Ranger platoon climbed up a 70 meter cliff in the middle of the night in the pouring rain to surprise and capture the German outpost there.

The Allies had intelligence informing them of a huge German gun battery at the tip of *Pointe du Hoc* that could shoot down onto the beaches, endangering thousands of allied lives. Many

Rangers sacrificed their lives to overrun the Germans, but in the end they found that the guns hadn't yet been installed. It was a futile effort, but man, they bombed the heck out of that place. The craters from bombers are still visible.

Photo Credit: www.normandybattlefields.com
Pointe du Hoc

In the gathering darkness we even got to the American graveyard. I ran everywhere because I had this feeling that, "I HAVE TO SEE." People had died there to make sure I could live free and that I could take part in adventures like the one I was currently undertaking, being an exchange student.

I would have liked to have gone to the German graveyard because I recognize that it's not only the Allies who fought courageously and died for their country, but by the time we got going again the stars were out.

The American Cemetery, Normandy

General Patton once said that you didn't win a war by dying for your country. Rather you won it by "making the other dumb bastard die for his country". However amusing that might be, I do think that respect is owed to both sides of the war. War isn't good for anybody, and I understood that more after being there. I saw it.

That day is one of the days I will remember for the rest of my life. I know it now, but I cannot express in words what this day means to me.

***

People tell me that I'm a skillful writer, but the only other time I wrote something long it was about a space-cowboy named Phil. I don't know how to express the feelings I have for what I experienced. I am not good enough to do that yet. Maybe I'll learn how to do it later, and then I'll write another book, better than this one. But for now I will have to make do with the skills I have today.

***

It was New Year's Eve, so we were lucky to find a little place to sleep in the countryside. The next day we woke up early and headed to *Ste. Mère Église*, where American airborne divisions had been dropped the night before the invasion. Unfortunately, one of the paratroopers landed and was caught on the spire of the church. He didn't die up there but was stranded for several hours and had some hearing loss due to the bells in the tower that sounded the arrival of the Americans.

They still have a mannequin up there to honor the brave American paratroopers who liberated Normandy that night.

Paratrooper hung up on the church steeple at *Ste. Mère Église*

After only a couple minutes in this town we moved on to *Carentan,* where Easy Company of the 101st Airborne Division took control of the city from the remaining Germans. The battle was beautifully depicted in the television series, "Band of Brothers," on HBO.

I had watched the beginning of the series before I left San Diego and was mad that I had not had time to finish it. I bought the book by Stephen Ambrose in the New York airport on the way to *France* and devoured it in a week.

After the book, I was even more unhappy that I had not had the chance to see the whole series, but now I was where it had actually happened.

***

Since it was still morning, we figured we had time to go to the *Mont St. Michèle*. If you don't know what that is, check out this picture.

Mont St. Michèle at low tide

It's basically a small island a couple hundred meters off of the Brittany coast which has a very small town and an old church on it. It looks like a sand castle. Everything is so compact that it is really fun to look at. The tides come and go faster than a man can run. We had to move our car by 5:30 PM because the parking lot was going to flood.

We ate lunch and walked around for a while. I stepped in dog crap, in a cemetery of all places, because there is no open space for a dog to do his business.

***

Believe it or not, we still had some time after that. Next we drove southeast toward *Paris* and got a room in a hotel in the city of *Chartres*. The next morning we walked over to what many people consider to be the most beautiful high gothic cathedral in the World.

You look up, and you believe it goes up to the heavens.

It's funny. It took more than 100 years to build the Cathedral of *Chartres.* All the while, the gothic style kept changing, so its two towers don't match.

The massive stained glass windows are like nothing else on Earth. Light pours into the interior, coloring the inside of the empty cathedral with an eerie light.

It's weird because you imagine this church as a place for lots of people and lots of prayer and lots of everything, but when we were there, there must have been a total of ten people in the church.

It was a dark winter morning, and the church was one of the only places to stay out of the cold.

It was amazing. Dad helped me brush up on my architectural skills by explaining the design and construction of flying buttresses as well as the stories depicted in the windows. This should help me in my Art History class when I get back to the U.S.

Chartres

Dad and I discussed what he knew and what I didn't, what I knew and he didn't, and after that we began a long drive back home to *Tournon*. We stopped for the night in *Dijon*, went to a movie and slept hard at the end of our own *tour de France*.

Back on the *autoroute* the next day. And luckily enough we arrived.

***

Yesterday I was going to school on my bike as normal. In my little town it's faster to be on a bike than to be in a car. I have a steep hill in front of my house, and at the bottom there is a bridge that takes you to the right.

I was going as fast as normal down the hill, which might be a tickle too fast, but I'll continue. At the bottom I looked to see if there was a car after the turn, meaning I would have to slow down. There wasn't, so I took the turn pretty hard.

I fell pretty hard, too. Did I tell you that it was -5° C, and the bridge was completely frozen?

It was actually a pretty cool fall because my back wheel just came out and I sat down and slid across into an ancient wall. I only got a hole in my pants, and it wasn't even that big.

That wasn't the first time I've ever fallen off a bike, and not the last either. This time I was lucky to come out unhurt. I only had some scabs, which is cool for picking up girls.

Later that same day, with a hole in my pants, I went to the ancient library at my school. I already told you my school is the oldest in *France*, dating from 1536. Back then there were two printing presses in my little town, and that made it one of the most important in *France*. Some of the first books ever made were printed in *Tournon*. I held books older than our American country. It was amazing. It really makes you think.

America is the little kid of world civilization. It's good to be reminded of it every once in a while. That's why Europeans flinch when they hear the word "American." We're "newbies." We know nothing of world history, the grand scheme of things.

People look at us as though we are trying to dominate the world when we should be leading it, even if we have holes in our pants.

Malloire

***

16 janvier 2002

Dear All,

I wanted to write you again to get back on schedule with my Wednesday afternoon break. I'm still recovering from the trip, but school has done me good. The house is all quiet after everybody who bunked here for the holidays has left. I miss the little kids (my host-parents' grandchildren, all as cute as anything), but I do admit that my life is much simpler now.

I put all the drawings they made for me in a collage of random things and pictures I have collected over the year. I have pictures of home and a lot of the people I miss from home. It is still a long time before I come home. I love being in *France*, but can't help thinking about coming home and seeing all my friends after such a long time. I wouldn't mind seeing photos of home, I'd put them up with the others.

Some people have told me that my French speaking level has gone down after speaking so much English with my Dad. Hopefully the next time I speak English it won't get worse because I would like to continue my progress.

I woke up at 6:00 to call my San Diego friend Mallory (except it's her first name and not my family name). I'm pretty exhausted, so I think I'll leave you and take a nap.

Malloire

Chapter 8
Break from the Ordinary

23 janvier 2002

Dear All,

I have a lot to tell you this week so settle in.

This last weekend was actually pretty cool. I had an AFS reunion, which sounds pretty torturous, but in fact it turned out to be pretty cool.

I arrived with a friend who will soon leave to spend a year in Alaska. Anyway, we arrived at 2:00 PM, like we were supposed to, at a *chateau* in *Annonay*, a nearby town, and nobody else showed up for an hour and a half.

I was thinking, "Oh, here we go. A whole weekend of this."

But everybody eventually did show up. I met with all the friends that I had made at the previous reunion, except the last reunion lasted two hours and this one would last two days.

I staked a claim on my bunk, put all my stuff down and took out a bunch of European candy. That stuff is awesome. Anyway, we talked with each other for two hours, and then we got into groups to evaluate our whole AFS experience and find out if we were actually happy or not.

Everybody from my group seemed to be happy campers, so that didn't last too long. We then ate what consisted of Asian sticky rice with tomato sauce mixed in. It was terrible.

After dinner we went back to our rooms, and I talked philosophy with a lovely Norwegian who speaks English fluently, but we ended up talking mostly in French. A bit of *"franglais."* I'm learning a little bit of French philosophy in school, and we talked about that and also serious matters like religion, sex, all that good stuff. Then we went back to the big main room where they had a CD player and a bunch of speakers, so we played a ton of music and danced until one o'clock. We danced cool Latin dances because there were a bunch of people from Central America.

I was glad I bunked with the people that I ended up with because we went straight to bed, while other people stayed up talking until four o'clock.

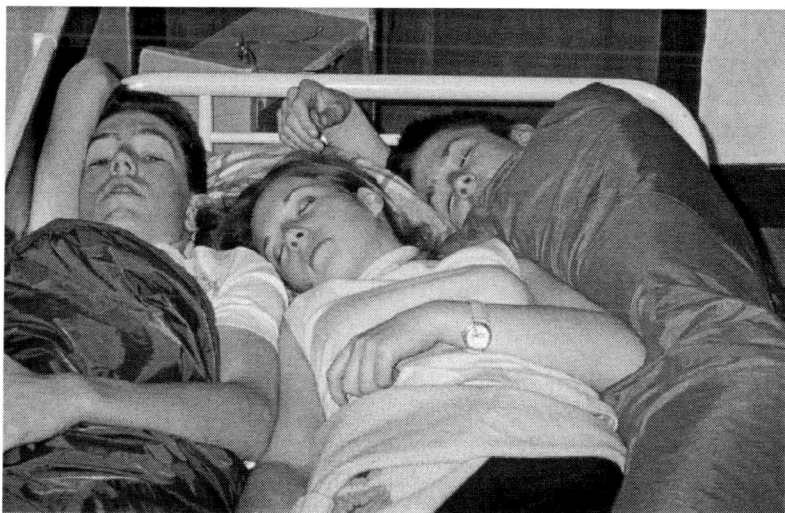

Gettin' a little friendly

Eight thirty was the time to get up. There wasn't a shower in my room, so we didn't get to take a shower like some others. We ate cereal for breakfast.

Then we prepared our skits to be presented to our host-parents. There were only eight guys and about twenty girls *(Tant mieux, n'est-ce pas?)* so the guys did *Popstars*, a popular French TV show that just ended, but there are only girls on the actual show.

The story line for our sketch was that there were five guys who were willing to humiliate themselves and who were competing to be the one AFStar. I was one of them.

There was one Venezuelan who was good at dancing, so she pretended to be our coach. We danced to Spice Girls, following what the Venezuelan was doing and then singing to "I Will Always Love You" by Whitney Houston.

Popstars

It was unimaginably funny for the AFS people, but I'm not sure about the parents. *Qu'est-ce que c'est que ce bordel?* Not my fault, peoples.

And then we ate *galettes des rois*. Basically it's a kind of pastry pie thing with ceramic figures baked inside and whoever gets the *roi* (king) in their piece means they win, and they get the little paper crown that comes with it.

Tera in her crown

Finally, we got to go home. My friend and I slept the entire way home. It had been an exhausting weekend. I made some friends and am planning on doing stuff with them outside the frame of AFS.

Thanks for reading. @+ !

Malloire

***

Some of the best friends I would make during my stay were made on AFS retreats. I had a connection with these people that didn't exist with my French friends. Like me, these people had left everything behind. We had come to a foreign country, and found each other. It is unbelievably meaningful and special.

Chapter 9
Sneezing and Training

30 janvier 2002

Dear All,

I went to bed without writing you. I woke up, realized that I hadn't written you, so I'm writing you now. You'll excuse me if I drift off topic.

This last weekend I was in the mountains of the *Ardèche* to train on my bike. I worked hard and found I was climbing especially well.

At times the forest got so thick that it was almost dark, with snow on both sides and moisture hanging in the air. On top of the mountain I could see *les Alps* in full splendor and also a mountain from which the *Loire* River (the biggest in *France*) gets its source. It was pretty cool.

It was a warm day, maybe eight degrees celsius, so it was nice to be outside again. Going up the mountains I was sweating a lot, but once I stopped I got cold again pretty quickly.

I went and bought a couple of French CD's today. Maybe that will get my host-Dad off my back about always playing music in English. Probably not.

I've got to go back to bed now.

Malloire

***

6 fevrier 2002

Dear All,

I hope you are doing well. For those of you who live in San Diego, I hope you're staying warm. In *France* there's a heat wave, so we're getting pretty decent temperatures.

Sunday I was again on my bike, this time in the rain. I was in a group, but we didn't go more than 55 kilometers. It's kind of miserable on a bike in the rain when it's five degrees outside. You get hungry, and start thinking, "What the fuck am I doing here?"

Just putting in my time, nothing more.

Monday I was again in a group, and we did a mountainous course. I'll say I wasn't the fastest, but then again I wasn't the slowest either. I'll start to really get back into it in another couple weeks.

Meanwhile, on to really big news. Yesterday I sneezed in History class.

That's not all I have to say, though. I pulled a muscle in between my ribs, and that really hurts. I'm trying to "nurse" myself back into health. I couldn't train on my bike today, but I hope that with a little luck I will get back to the norm soon.

I have to excuse myself, for I no longer write in "good English." On an English test last week I scored only 17 out of 20. Some of you will say that it's a B, but no. The average score in my English class is 10 and 20 is unattainable. It's just the French system.

Anyway my English wants to deform into French and I say things like, "under the rain" or "he is doctor" which, directly translated, is the French way of saying of saying "in the rain" and "he is a doctor." It'll be interesting when I get back, I'm sure.

Malloire

***

8 fevrier 2002

(To John Howard, my cycling coach via the Internet)

John,

I'd like to visit a friend the around the 20th of February. She says she's free during the week (it's vacation for us) so I'd like to go see her on my bike. The hitch is that she lives 87 kilometers away. It's all flat, though.

Last year I did huge rides with my Dad, going up to Dana Point to eat, which works out to be 170 kilometers round trip. I was thinking that I could start in the morning, then eat lunch with her, and then leave. That would make a good 174 kilometers, or about 120 miles. I'm pretty confident that I could do it just on plain stubbornness, but I haven't done a ton of kilometers yet.

I'm asking you which day I should do it, or if it would screw things up, that I shouldn't do it. Thanks.

Malloire

***

John Howard was my cycling coach in San Diego and while I was in *France*. He's a really famous guy, Pan American Champion Cyclist, Hawaii Ironman Champion. He even set the World Land Speed Record for bicycles at over 150 mph. It's cool to be able to ride with someone who has been so many places with his bike.

Throughout my year in France I had an ongoing relationship with John and cleared all of my training with him. He would send me charts and calendars and advice on stretching. He gave me a schedule that I could follow so that I would finally be able to climb *le Mont Ventoux*. It's not just a hill you can decide to go up on a whim. You have to train religiously for many months before you can do it. I was making an effort to do just that.

***

Reading through this book, it may sound like I get to do a lot of stuff and that I don't really spend much time training on my bike. *Au contraire*, I spend hours sitting on a tiny saddle "limping" home after climbing mountains that normal people need nothing to do with.

I am not normal. I am a bike racer. I am devoted. When I say I'm training for *le Ventoux* I'm not just walking to school and back and then saying to myself, "Oh, what a good boy am I?"

I am hardcore.

People don't always know what to say or how to understand, and that's fine with me because I know that in some ways I am better than they are.

Maybe that's all it comes down to. I want to be better than other people. I'm competitive in everything. So this whole deal with *le Ventoux* is personal. I am striving to prove that I am better than whatever *les Alps* can put in front of me.

***

13 fevrier 2002

Dear All,

I hope you are all well. You'd tell me if you weren't, wouldn't you?

It started to rain here last night, and basically it hasn't stopped. I was on my bike this afternoon in a *peloton* and it was actually a little bit nice, with not too much wind for two and a half hours, but then for the last half hour it started pouring, and the wind kicked up. Everybody started hauling butt because it sucks to be soaking wet and cold at the same time.

And on Monday, the wind was so strong that to pedal was a little pointless when the wind was with you. But going the other direction was agony. And the crosswinds are really strong because there aren't any trees to control the wind when you're in the country with all the farms.

All in a day's work, though.

I don't have much else to tell you. My French teacher says I'm making progress. I also lost a badminton match today in PE.

That sums it up.

Gotta Go! @+

Malloire

Chapter 10
The Sun Doesn't Shine in *Paris*

17 fevrier 2002

Dear All,

I hope you are all doing well.

I just got back from *Paris*. I stayed there six days during a two-week February vacation when everybody in *France* goes skiing. Except right now the skiing isn't great because of the high temperatures.

First of all I went to *Paris* on the *"train grande vitesse."* At 300 kph it's kind of scary when another *TGV* passes because the wind knocks the trains to the side and for a couple of seconds there's an annoying noise screaming from all around.

But all in all it's pretty cool. It's not too different from a plane except there aren't any seatbelts or flight attendants.

In *Paris* I really didn't see too much. I slept a lot and recovered from school and cycling. I stayed with an absolutely lovely family. *Jean-Claude Oeud* is a very well educated and genuinely intelligent man who loves to learn things and teach them to others.

He is an unbelievably kind man with a great handshake and a strong gaze. His wife is quite different. She is smart and witty but sometimes she gets mad, and you don't know if she's joking or not. Then she reveals a kind of a "smirk," which is only occasionally reassuring.

They were lovely people and I'm grateful to know them.

Jean-Claude Oeud

I ate well and in large quantities, and I did manage to get around a bit. I saw the *Chateau de Versailles*, built by *Louis XIV* to outdo all of the other *chateaux* in *France*.

He succeeded.

It was a saddening experience because two or three years ago a huge storm swept through *Europe* and knocked a ton of trees down in the gardens of *Versailles*. These trees were all huge, looming monuments. Now the trees are small and sad-looking. There's construction all around and no flowers, and in addition it was raining.

In fact, I never saw the sun the whole time I was in *Paris*. Sometimes I could tell that the sun was right behind those clouds over there. It was really making a concerted effort to get through, but to no avail.

Sad, but I enjoyed myself.

On *le Metro* (subway) I imagined I was a student like all the others I saw, just going to class. Except taking *le Metro*. I tried to imagine it all being banal and tiresome, but it was still exciting in my head.

I liked that thought. Or at least I used the time on the train for a cool subject.

I also bought some things and saw a car expo. I bought a picture of the 1968 GT sports car race looking down a long straight at the Nurburgring in Germany.

If you understood that last sentence, just know that you're cool. If you didn't, you're cool in your own way, don't worry.

Gotta Go!

Malloire

***

20 fevrier 2002

Dear All,

I hope you are all doing well.

My life has been busier on vacation than when I'm going to school. Right now I'm on my second week of vacation. It'll calm down starting tomorrow.

My host-parents' grandkids have just left, so I finally have time to write you. There were three of them, going from two and a half to eight. It was a circus here. I don't understand how some kids can have so many toys and play with only one while all the time spreading the other toys around the house. I really just don't get it.

I saw the new *Asterix* and *Obelix* movie. *Asterix* and *Obelix* are Gauls, the inhabitants of *France* during Roman times. It's a famous cartoon series and comic book in *Europe*, and it was recently made into two movies.

These movies are awesome. It's refreshingly funny for little kids, with little or no real violence. The thing about *Asterix* and *Obelix* is that they know a guy named *Panoramix*, who makes a magic potion giving them almost infinite power.

So *Asterix* and *Obelix* go around scaring the Romans and have fun doing it. It's a great story.

Anyway when I went to the movie theater I saw a little story before. I have no idea if this story exists in the U.S., but I saw it in French and have translated it for you below:

An old man, in the middle of the desert, sits and looks at his failed farm. He is skinny, with his miserable income he doesn't get to eat too often. He lives in the smallest of towns, just he and his neighbor, a neighbor not well liked by this old man.

He was so sad that he prayed to heaven and hell to give him a wish. But it was hell who finally promised to grant him his wish, in exchange for an eternity with the small man with the pointy tail, and on one condition, that his neighbor get twice of whatever he wishes for.

The old man accepted. But what did he want?

He thought to himself, "A good farm might do." But he remembered that his neighbor would have two good farms. No, that doesn't work.

A good crop, but no! His neighbor would have two.

A sack of gold would give the same predicament. He thought through the night, and the next morning the small man with the pointy tail came to take the old man's decision.

And the old man simply replied, "Take my right eye."

Kind of scary but it makes you think. I liked it.

That's all for this week.

Soyez sages les enfants.

Malloire

Chapter 11
Hypo #3

27 fevrier 2002

Dear All,

I hope you are all doing well.

School has been good to me these last three days. I handed in the homework I did on vacation and I had fun. But on Sunday I had a little bit of a problem on my bike.

I woke up early to be able to get my training in before lunch, when the day really starts. It was around 5° C, not too cold. I didn't put on many clothes because I knew I would be climbing, and then when the time came to turn around hopefully it would be warmer.

It didn't work out the way I wanted it to.

I climbed, and after about 30 minutes it started to rain lightly. I thought about turning around and getting rain gear but decided against it.

I kept on climbing and climbing. I got to *St. Félicien* (a small town in the mountains of the *Ardèche*) and made the turn to conquer *le Col du Buisson*.

It's a good-sized climb, maybe around 13 kilometers, but because I'd already climbed 27 kilometers that day, it wasn't going to be a problem.

I started and noticed for really the first time that I was wet. Being wet and being cold come hand-in-hand. I'm stubborn, at least on the bike, so I continued.

Four kilometers from the top it started to snow. It levels out a little bit for the last 4 kilometers so I decided to just put my head down and get there.

I got to the top, put my hands in my armpits to warm them for a little bit, and then turned around in the direction of home.

HOLY CRAP I got cold!

It was amazingly cold, and because I was wearing my smaller sized gloves, my hands were ready to go on strike and take a vacation.

Also, I couldn't feel my feet anymore.

I started to shake and swerve across the road. Luckily, I got all the way down the *col* in one piece, but I was going very slowly around the turns. I knew how easily I could fall and slide off the road. My goodness!

I got back to *St. Félicien*. I decided that I could make it home, and everything would be all right.

I kept going, but shortly afterwards I realized I would have to stop as soon as possible. Unfortunately, the next village was a little further than I anticipated.

I stopped at a small store that my host-parents knew. I used their phone to call home and sat down and shook violently while they were on their way. It was scary.

That's the third time in my life I've had hypothermia, but by far the best story. The other two times I was playing soccer and rowing in the rain.

That afternoon after *Jean-Claude* had picked me up we went to a wine festival (because we live in a wine region). I tasted lots of different wines . . . to warm up, you know.

Anyway I had to buy a bottle of wine for my host-Dad because the Winter Olympics were on and the French came first and second in the Men's Slalom, and the good American guy fell. I was sad.

The wine was good though.

That's all, at least for now.

Malloire

***

During the Olympics there was a lot of rivalry and betting going on. I won on a few occasions, but seemed to lose on more.

***

6 March 2002

Dear All,

I hope you're all doing well. I have been the happiest I've been in a while. School is awesome, I am more open to people and they're more open with me. I feel a ton more comfortable.

I also had an AFS weekend, and it was great. I sang a song with my good friend Froger (that's his last name.) He played the guitar and I and a couple of other people sang.

It was the second best thing at the AFS weekend "talent show." The coolest thing was a good German fellow named Sebastian, who played the flute like a maniac. It was really quite amazing.

***

I've done a lot more cycling this week and I just got back from conquering the ride I tried to do before I got hypothermia. I actually had done all the hard work before I had to stop, so it was just a descent afterwards.

***

I really can't tell you much more. I have to continue on this path full of cool things.

Before this week I wanted to come home and see all my friends but now it's like, "I can't go home. It's just not possible. I need more time."

But be sure that I'll be glad to see you when I do finally get home. I love you all.

Malloire

***

Of course it was all about a girl, this high that I was feeling. There's not much more to say because that's about as long as it lasted, unfortunately. She wasn't the person I thought she was. I was actually used.

It happens.

Chapter 12
Getting Back on Track

13 mars 2002

Dear All,

I hope you're all doing well.

I've finally started to feel good doing what I do best, riding my bike. I'm getting known around town as "that American who rides his bike like the pros." I've been climbing well on the bike for the first time in my life.

Here a short hill is five kilometers. In San Diego it's 50 meters. The difference here is amazing. I'm doing great and feeling really in my niche. It's like I've found what I was meant to do.

Sunday my parents went skiing without me. I stayed home and managed cooking dinner and doing all the cool things just like at home.

I ate well, I put the music on nice and loud, basically I just had a cool time. It reminded me a bit of the independent life I have at home in the States. I wouldn't say that I miss that life, but it does have its advantages. I had the opportunity to make decisions again, since that was kind of something that AFS has taken away from me.

Meanwhile, it has gotten unbelievably hot here. I'm going around in a T-shirt almost all the time. It's maybe 18° C. That's got to be so cold for you, but for me it's burning up.

I'll get my San Diego tan back soon, maybe. I just hope that I won't stay so pasty.

Malloire

Chapter 13
Why?

20 mars 2002

Dear All,

I hope you're all doing well.

I felt like I've done a lot this last week. I rode my bike, but not as much as I might have liked. I had my reasons though.

On Sunday my host-parents and I went to eat lunch with this charming couple and their good friends. The man of the house was actually paralyzed. He's an awesome guy. He doesn't talk much, but you can see things in his eyes that you can't see in yours or mine.

For some reason I'm petrified of becoming like him. He scares the crap out of me. I have accidents on my bike way too often, and one of those times could be the accident that puts me in a wheelchair for the rest of my life.

I honor and respect this man, but at the same time he scares me.

My last bike accident was traumatic. I guess I'll tell you the story because you haven't heard it.

I was in a friendly training race in San Diego and in a rather large *peloton* (group of cyclists.) I was hanging towards the back to save my energy in the draft when two guys in front of me fell. I fell right after.

Like a large majority of my accidents it wasn't my fault. I lost consciousness for a couple of minutes, and now remember asking the English paramedic if he was Australian about four times.

I went to the hospital in an ambulance and spent the night and most of the next morning there. I didn't realize it at the time, but that scared the heck out of me.

I realized that every day could be my last, that I might not live until I'm 100 years old and die in my sleep. I'm guessing that this is a helpful discovery, but I feel vulnerable and almost weak. I've discovered that I don't have the power that I thought I had.

For those of you who are young and haven't yet gone down this path, make sure to make the best out of your life. I'll do my best with mine.

Until next week,

Malloire

***

I currently have a poster of James Dean on my wall. I do not admire him for his "Rebel Without a Cause" reputation or his mind-frame, but more for something he said.

He said, "Dream as if you'll live forever; live as if you'll die today."

Take advantage of your life, it's the only one you got. Doesn't that sound corny, though?

Let's think about this. Our Moms would probably keep us inside all the time, not exposing us to germs or passing cars or bee-stings or skydiving or soccer or whatever makes life dangerous. But what some do not realize is that things that aren't risky or challenging aren't worth doing.

Why can't we have challenge and fun in our lives? Why would we spend our lives not living them in a noble, exciting way?

All of us have to find what makes us happy and fulfilled, but too many people compromise what they care about for things like money, power, or prestige.

I say, "Do what you love first, and if you love it enough, everything else will fall into line." I'm in the process of trying all this out, so get back to me in a couple years.

E-mail is philipmallory1@hotmail.com. Hopefully it won't change.

Chapter 14
I Would Walk 5,000 Miles

27 mars 2002

Dear All,

I hope you are all doing well.

I'm about to set off on an adventure. This Thursday and Friday as part of a school event I'm going to walk 40 kilometers in snowshoes in the mountains not far from my house. I'm preparing everything right now, so the house is kind of a mess.

I'm going to take pictures and have fun with my friends. It seems like it will be pretty cool. I really don't have much to say, but next week I definitely will.

Until then,

Malloire

***

3 avril 2002

Dear All,

I hope you are all doing well.

The last time I sent an e-mail I said that I was going to the mountains to walk with some snowshoes. It didn't work out like that. I did walk 45 kilometers, but there was no snow.

It was one of the hardest things that I have ever done.

The first day was toughest because I had 15 kilos on my back, and I was wearing hiking boots that didn't belong to me.

I have really narrow feet, so I was sliding back and forth inside the shoes. When I finally had the chance to take my shoes off, I had to get my knife out to work on my blisters. Luckily I had a couple of Band-Aids to put on the next day.

That whole day I tried to eat as much as I could to lighten my load, but at the end I couldn't notice much improvement.

I spent most of the day talking to people at the front of the line we formed, but as we were coming to the last couple of kilometers I was hanging out with the fat kids at the back, and pretty soon I was hanging out with myself. I was terribly tired.

We slept in a refuge in the middle of nowhere. Normally if you bring 30 teenagers together at a hotel, or in our case a refuge, you don't get much sleep. *Au contraire*. I slept a good twelve hours. Everybody was exhausted.

The next morning I put on an extra pair of socks to compensate for the width of my shoes. It worked out pretty well, but almost immediately we hiked up 600 meters, not in distance but in elevation.

It was really, really hard. We climbed above the tree line. I didn't eat enough, so by the last 200 meters I was absolutely lost in hurt. My backpack had me off balance, and it was so steep that I almost fell a couple of times. I managed to continue only by holding onto the grass that survived where trees couldn't.

There was a lot of snow up there, but it was melting snow. That said, everything was muddy and slippery. I had barely made it up the last 200 meters, but it was worth it. We were on top of everything around us. I looked down cliffs plunging down to what looked like legos or something.

I could see farms and tiny towns below me. It was one of
the coolest things I'd ever seen. Sure, you could see the same kind
of thing from an airplane, but I knew that I myself had conquered

This was exactly what I expect of my ride to *le Ventoux*, except I wanted it to be harder and more special. I want my climb to mean everything to me. I feel that if I make it up all the way my entire trip to France will be worthwhile, that all the physical hardship will be secondary to the psychological triumph.

It's more than a mountain.

I feel I can do anything I set my mind to physically, but psychologically I had things to prove to myself. The only way I could do that was to challenge myself and take physical risks.

We found a wind-sheltered place to eat lunch when, from behind a cliff without the slightest bit of noise, a motorized glider surged up and above us.

This glider was using a tiny motor and the updrafts in front of the cliffs to climb up to us. It couldn't have been more than 50 meters from us when it appeared. I had spent four hours and most of my energy climbing this staggering mountain, only to be outdone in seconds by man's innovation. It was mind-blowingly awesome, one of the coolest experiences of my life.

Some day I will fly like that.

Coming back down the mountain there were bands of snow. We took out our plastic garbage bags and slid down until we fell or until the hill stopped. Serious mountaineers call this *glissade*, but to us, it was amazingly funny to watch huge guys rolling down a hill at 50 kph.

***

Anyway, the hour has changed here and not in San Diego, so for the moment there are ten hours of time delay.

I had a really cool Easter, and school vacation is upon me, only two more days.

Spring is in full swing here, flowers everywhere and leaves getting back on the trees. It's getting warmer and will soon be ideal for cycling again, before it gets too hot.

I'm feeling awesome here. I only need to train a little more on the bike to be really happy. The spring break will be a great opportunity before climbing *l'Alpe d'Huez* and *le Mont Ventoux*, the two most famous climbs anywhere.

See Ya,

Malloire

Chapter 15
Training

10 avril 2002

Dear All,

I hope you are all doing well.

I'm riding a lot on my bike. I'm happy to get back to something I know and love. I'm on vacation right now so I can get a lot of kilometers on my legs.

This last Saturday I did 120 kilometers with a large *peloton* at full speed through the mountains. Yesterday I did 110 kilometers just cruising, but I did it alone, so I had to fight alone against the wind.

On my Sunday ride I passed through the small town of *Nozières*, and normally nobody is in the main square. This time there was a ton of people. They were coming out of the church, and they were all very nicely dressed, so when somebody walked near me while I was eating a Powerbar, I asked him if it was a wedding.

He replied, "No, a funeral."

Obviously, I felt pretty bad.

Today I did a *peloton* ride of 60 kilometers, but it started to rain and got a lot colder, so everybody hurried home to the comfort of dry clothes and warm houses.

***

Once when I was riding in San Diego with the San Diego Bike Club *peloton*, and it was raining. A guy asked why it was that whenever the conditions weren't great that everyone was hungry.

He seemed to really be considering what psychological influences the weather had on you.

I simply told him that it was because your subconscious was yelling at you saying, "Why the hell am I out here?" Pretty simple, really. Nobody likes to be miserable.

He laughed.

***

At the end of these two weeks of vacation I'm going to climb *l'Alpe d'Huez*, a huge climb that is often included in the *Tour de France* and climbs up to the ski station where I had already skied twice.

I'm climbing up there the last ski day of the ski season. I'm going with the ski club in *Tournon*. They're going to bring me most of the way with the bike on the bus in with the skis, and then 50 kilometers from the ski station they'll tell me, *"Au Revoir,"* and I'll see them up again at the top.

And I'm going to do it on my new and early birthday present, for my birthday is May 1st for those of you who have forgotten. *(Pensez aux cadeaux!)* Dad let me buy another *Look* bike, this one for training. I have selected a carbon fiber frame because carbon lasts a lot longer than aluminum.

Now we'll have two good bikes to ride when Dad comes this summer. The lowest gear on the new bike is 30 teeth in front and 23 in back. That should suit Dad just fine.

***

I listen to a ton of music here in *France*. I'm climbing out of my Clapton phase and plunging into my Zeppelin phase. I've heard Zeppelin all my life practically, but for the first time it's become important. "Rain Song" is magic. It makes me want to know how to play the guitar.

Until next week,

Malloire

***

My taste in music really did transform in *France*, and I thought that it was a reflection of how much I had changed. I loved old stuff like Zeppelin and had a real respect for it just like I have a respect for that generation. But now I also listen to new stuff that I had never listened to before, which shows how I was becoming adventurous and daring.

Maybe I'm looking into it too much, though.

Probably.

Chapter 16
Whoa the *Stylo!*

24 avril 2002

Dear All,

I hope you are all doing well.

I haven't written for two weeks, not because I had nothing to say, but because I lacked the motivation to write a long letter.

A lot has recently happened in *France*. There was the first round of the presidential elections, and a dangerous man from the far right named *Jean-Marie Le Pen* was advanced to the run-off along with current president *Jacques Chirac*.

A lot of people were outraged, and from what I've gathered, were ashamed of the French people. *Le Pen* is a man who opposes all immigration and wants to keep "*France* for the French," a code word for racism in any language, any culture.

Anyway, he accomplished the task he set out for himself because he has become a legitimate politician in the eyes of much of the public. It was really astounding that this horrible, dangerous man could achieve what he had. The youth and much of the French community wanted to fight back.

So my high school went to the streets yesterday, myself included.

We protested and let everybody know about it. It was an amazing experience for me because I don't see that ever happening in San Diego.

Kids at home aren't aware of what happens politically, and even if they were, they don't seem to care enough to get involved, maybe because they think they wouldn't make a difference.

I disagree with the fascists and the communists, but I do still believe that their presence in *France* is a healthy one, although dangerous.

To make a long story short, everybody cut morning classes and went to the streets. It was completely legal, and even the police were there just to make sure we didn't do anything stupid.

We walked in the street and made a complete traffic mess to express our civil liberties. But at the same time I think this opportunity was abused to a certain extent. People who didn't want to go to class didn't, while for others it was a noble cause.

Tomorrow there are more protests, but I've been told by AFS not to go. I like following the rules, but I don't know what I'm going to do tomorrow. I don't have classes, so I could easily do it, but I'd be out of my element, being an American.

What impact would I have? Who would even care about what I think? Nobody likes foreigners, right?

***

School here is winding down. We don't have much more than a month. People in my class are getting nervous because there are big tests at the end of the year, and they have to study.

A friend of mine told me that he would gladly take my place. He'd love to be an American so he wouldn't have to take the tests, but I immediately told him that I have my own troubles at home to worry about.

***

It has been absolutely beautiful here. San Diego weather has come to visit. It continues to get hotter and hotter, but it's still chilly in the morning. As it gets warmer I have to breathe in air that's warmer. I find that without cold air rushing into my mouth like it did just a little while ago, I feel like not breathing.

The air is so hot and disgusting. I want cold air. I breathe in really quickly so that the air feels cold, but that's tiring and makes your head feel a little tipsy.

I got a little more accustomed to the cold weather than I expected, I guess.

***

With the nice weather I've ridden my bike a lot and actually rode 140 kilometers with the *peloton* on Saturday. I felt good, but the last 25 kilometers I was falling behind, and my shoulders were killing me.

I felt good about my effort and will continue to do well and keep on schedule.

Until next week,

Malloire

***

I did forget to add something to this letter. Maybe it was because I was so livid. I did not get the chance to ride up *l'Alpe d'Huez,* like I had planned. The ski club decided that since I would be riding on their bus, that they would be liable for me, and I would be breaking the rules of AFS anyway. Well, it meant enough to me that I was willing to take the risk. I was achieving goals!

I certainly hoped I wouldn't get hurt, and I would do my best to see that it never happens, but I was frustrated that people couldn't see how much this meant to me. I would be filling the shoes of the giant cycling competitors who had come to conquer this mountain before me.

Why wouldn't all these people just let me be? If they were so concerned about me then they should have seen the importance this had.

But it's past. What's done is done.

I have nothing more to say.

Chapter 17
B-Day

1 mai 2002

So it's my birthday. May Day.

Moi with neighbor *Michelle* and *Maman Lou-Lou*

I haven't celebrated my birthday for many, many years. Your birthday is just another day, and I feel that you don't get a year older you get a day older, and so celebrating your birthday is kind of not worth it if you don't celebrate each and every day for what it is.

I guess I try to do that. I succeed in some ways, fail in others. It's important that you try to succeed in every single day. Take things one day at a time. If you can get through one day, you can get through the next. It's an ideal, and most people will say, "Yeah, that sounds good," but it will go right past them.

That's not necessarily bad, but it's unfortunate.

Age just isn't all that important to me. Some people have lived longer lives, I feel, and they are no older than I am. Others haven't lived much at all, even after 20 or 30 years. But it all just depends on what you do and how you make your life. You are the "architect" of your own destiny.

So that was my birthday philosophical spiel.

Thanks for listening.

Malloire

Chapter 18
Ventoux Massacre

This was something that I never wrote about in a letter home. It was too hard for me at the time. I didn't want to admit defeat. I don't like losing.

So what happened? I guess I'll tell you since I've gotten this far.

On *11 mai 2002* I went to climb *le Mont Ventoux*.

My parents and I drove about four hours South down the *Rhône*, until the valley opened into the wide Mediterranean plain of *Provence*. They understood how important it was to me.

In *Tournon* there are forests to ride through to keep me in the shade, away from the sun. In *Provence* the forests have been cleared centuries ago. Now mostly there are bushes and shrubs.

Bushes suck compared to trees.

There are rows and rows of grape vines, the kind that are so much fun to look down when you're passing perpendicular in a car. Every so often there are rosebushes between the vineyards.

It's pretty, but it's so much hotter here. It's windier. There's no protection, even on a cloudy day like today.

It's a rolling but mostly flat countryside. It's *Provence.* Hot and unpleasant, more like Italy than *France,* with a piercing Mediterranean sun. *Van Gogh* painted in *Provence,* said the light was like nowhere else in France. I believe it.

Photo Credit: CyberFrance

And then over my shoulder is *le Ventoux.* They say it's part of *les Alps,* but it is so far from *les Alps* in so many ways.

Les Alps I know are perfectly picturesque all year round, with jagged, snow-capped peaks stretching to the clouds, with cows in meadows and villages with church spires. *Le Ventoux* is one solitary, smooth and round mountain set far apart from all the other mountains it's size.

It's hot and white and bare.

It's alone, out of place.

It sits on the landscape like a scoop of ice cream half melted in the Mediterranean sun, a shape that looks oddly alive, organic.

Since I wanted it to be the hardest thing I've ever done, I started my ride in the village of *Bolléne*, 50 kilometers from the start of the climb. Little did I know....

Maman Lo-Lou posing with me in *Bolléne*

My host-parents dropped me off and raced ahead of me and ate at a restaurant. I carried some food and ate a little on the way, but I didn't get a full meal in. Unfortunately, I weighed maybe 50 kilos at the time, and did not have any physical reserves.

Not eating more was stupid. There's no other way to put it.

Past the village of *Bédoin* I begin my approach to the mountain. You know, it's really not that bad. For around four kilometers after *Bédoin* I pass through farm fields and past a small church.

Photo Credit: grenoblecycling.free.fr

Now I'm in the pine forest that covers the lower slopes of the mountain.

Photo Credit: Russ Collins

I look up at the summit way in front of me. I say to myself that if the rest continues the way that it was going so far, then I would make it to the top no problem. Little did I know....

Then I go around a blind hairpin turn, and the road kicks up to 10+% in steepness.

Oops. I guess this is the real start of the ascent. I say to myself, "It'll level out pretty soon." I'm not too worried.

Three kilometers later, when it has gotten only steeper, I'm beginning to doubt myself. It's slow going. Really slow going.

Why is this going so slow? I am going up *le Ventoux*. It's

pretty. It's warm but not too so. My equipment is turning over and over. I'm on my smallest chain ring. The road is following a meandering gully up the slope. Every kilometer there is another stone marker with the road gradient. 8.8%. 9.2%.

It's quiet, being completely alone in this forest. Why is it so quiet? Why do I find myself stopping on this mountain I have dreamed about for so long? It's only been ten kilometers since the climb started. I had felt great before beginning the climb.

What's going on? Why are my legs shot?

I keep clicking over. My parents stop every kilometer marker up the mountain and watch me go by before racing ahead again in the car.

Then I hit the wall. Just like that.

My host-parents stop me. *Jean-Claude* has noticed that I took much too long over the last kilometer. He realizes I'm not going to make it.

I get off the bike, leaning it up against the car. I sit down in the shade, eat a banana and watch my dream slipping away right in front of my watering, blurry eyes.

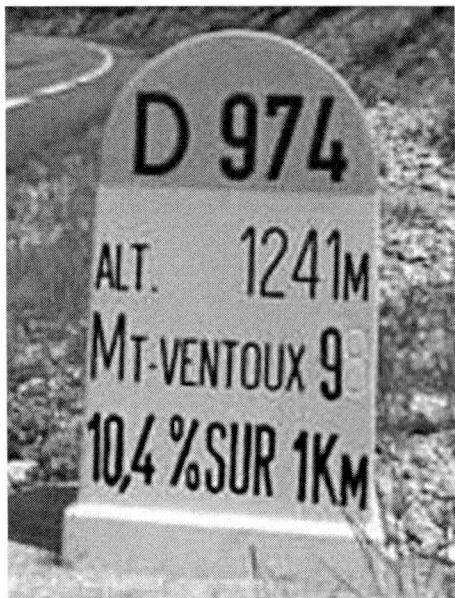

I look at the stone marker beside me. Nine kilometers and 668 vertical meters to go. It's shaped like a tombstone. I never noticed before.

This is the first time I cried since Normandy. I sat down all by myself and cried, feeling so lonely against this mountain that had defeated me.

Why wasn't I strong enough? I had been doing things right.

But it didn't matter. I lost.

At least we could keep driving, out of the forest and onto the bare moonscape leading to the mountain top.

This is more than a mountain.

People have died on this bald mountain. I just died mentally on this mountain.

In the summer heat of the 1967 *Tour de France*, Tom Simpson, 1965 World Road Champion, the finest cyclist Britain has ever produced, found his date with destiny up here, only a couple of kilometers from the summit.

It was the 13th stage, held on Friday, July 13th. Simpson battled mightily on the slopes of the mountain that day, but after more than ten kilometers he began to slip behind the lead group. Soon he was weaving across the road.

He toppled from his bicycle, and when spectators came to his aid, he gasped, "Put me back on my bike."

Those were his last words. He died right there at the side of the road, above the tree line, amid the hot white rocks that make the mountain look snow-capped from a distance.

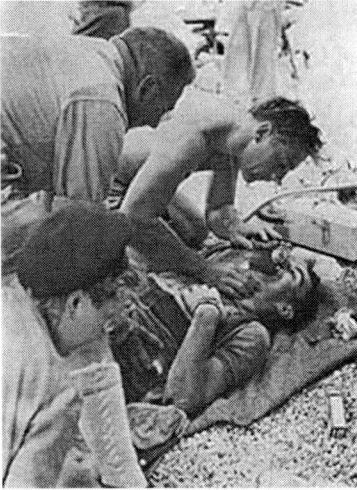

"I'm not nearly as good as Tom Simpson was," I thought to myself. But then again, 40 years ago Tom Simpson had a very odd idea about how best to prepare himself before tackling *le Mont Ventoux*.

Before my own next assault on *le Ventoux*, I won't be taking amphetamines and drinking half a bottle of cognac in a bar at the foot of the climb, like Mr. Simpson did that last day of his life.

For future reference: Don't take amphetamines and drink half a bottle of anything but water before climbing any mountain.

There's a monument to Tom Simpson on the spot where he died. I stopped and paid my respects.

Then for the first time I got to see close-up the final mound that marks the summit of *le Mont Ventoux*.

Photo Credit: Antonie Venema

In the last 25 meters the road kicks up and encircles a weather station perched on the very top of this very round mountain.

"I'll be back," I promise myself.

Chapter 19
Catching Up

24 mai 2002

Dear All,

I hope you are all doing well.

I haven't written in a while, I've been unbelievably busy doing as little as possible. I've been riding my bike a lot, reading good books, doing some schoolwork (emphasis on some), and watching the world around me change for the better.

When I was younger (as if I'm not young now), I was never happy when I was alone. I have come to appreciate time spent alone, doing what I want to do. But at the same time I am willing to make sacrifices when other people are around me. Being alone has some sort of complete liberty to it, but when I am with others I try to do what makes the people around me happy, because when the most important people in my life are happy, I can't help but be glad about it.

During the last month I haven't written you, but I've learned a lot and done even more. The simplest and maybe most enjoyable thing that I have done is to have watched a wonderful, eventful spring develop around me.

Spring is a wonderful thing. There are now leaves on the trees where once they were naked, cherries on the cherry trees providing food for us animals and good feelings for all, grass one meter tall, and more insects that I have ever seen or killed in my entire life.

If you like cherries, you should come visit. I spend hours outside. At 8:30 PM I'm watching the sunset while picking cherries three to four meters off the ground.

It's a peaceful life. There's no music, but you can listen to the leaves in the wind. I wouldn't mind if it rained, I would just be forced to come to the conclusion that I would get wet and it would be harder for me to get down.

My fingers are sore from twisting the cherries off of the branches. I've picked more than 20 kilos.

I spend hours avoiding the firmness and safety we call ground. I enjoy myself. It's unbelievably simple; it's beautiful in a way.

And I don't even like cherries.

***

Between the poetic pauses I seem to stumble upon every day, I participated in three bike races. I had a cool time doing them. Some people think that since I think so much that I would lack the intensity it requires to race and be competitive enough to bite someone's head off. This isn't true. I am fierce, and you better not be in my way.

***

The first race, *la Cinquième Ronde Donatiènne*, was a great one. We did about 40 kilometers before several very good senior women and another junior man made a breakaway. At three kilometers to go, I chased after them to bridge the gap. The *peloton* seemed exhausted and didn't follow me.

I joined the back of the breakaway and stayed in the protection of their draft until the final climb of about 200 meters.

We got to the climb, and everybody spread out across the road. I said to myself, "Why the heck are we going so slowly?" I thought maybe a sprint would be launched at any moment, but the slow pace continued. I tried to get to the front, but with everybody strewn across the road, I couldn't get by.

I said some precise words in French, and one lady slid to the side a fraction, just enough for me to get by. I sprinted ahead of everybody and discovered that I had made some distance with 100 meters still to the line.

It continued as a false flat all the way to the finish, and I felt like I was going much too slow and hurting much too much.

The finish line approached ever so slowly. I didn't look behind. I just put my head down and pushed for the line.

When I looked around, I discovered that I was 40 meters ahead of everybody else and probably could have cruised to the line, but I didn't have the courage to look behind me. Thank goodness.

I pedaled a bit and then went back to the finish line. Some lady said in French, "There's that skinny kid who kicked everybody else's ass." I pretended I didn't hear, but I smiled to myself.

My first race in *France* had been conquered, and I came out on top.

***

The second race was really hard, with lots less luck. I found myself behind, really busting my butt in a small chase group 400 meters behind a guy that I easily tossed to the side in the race two weeks earlier.

Nobody in my group was helping me set the pace, so when we got close enough I dropped them and bridged up to the leader.

Now it was just between the two of us. It was unbelievably windy, and he was heavier than me. I obviously had much more experience than he did, but he was more muscular, so I sat on his wheel to protect myself from the wind and let him tire himself out.

Apparently it worked. On the last climb to the finish he led out the sprint, and ten meters from the line I burst ahead and took the victory with style.

Just like the first time I stayed and collected my trophy, and then everybody left. I was still there, looking around the bend, assuring myself that my host-Dad was right around it and he would pop out and pick me up.

I got kind of worried when it started to get dark. A nice man from a group of cyclists who actually put on the race and who stayed behind drinking alcohol lent me his cell phone. *Jean-Claude* had indeed forgotten about me, and it was a 45-minute drive from *Tournon*. I wasn't too surprised, but at the same time I wasn't frustrated. I had won again.

Me after drinking *champagne* from my trophy

***

For the third race, *le 23e Grand Prix Cycliste de Tain-l'Hermitage, sur la Montée de Larnage*, it was pouring rain, absolutely disgusting. Someone drew an extra line on the sign for the race, turning the "L" into a "C," so it truly was *le Montée de Carnage*.

In the rain I was all alone in the junior category, since nobody else wanted to show up, but I was successful in lapping my imaginary competitor because he got a flat. His name was Bob. Apparently Lady Luck can't see invisible people.

For this race I got my photo in the regional paper. They left out that I was all alone in my category, but they did say: *"A noter encore la belle place du jeune coureur américain du Friol Club Philippe Mallory qui arrive premier dans la categorie cadet, certainment un futur Astromg."*

Certainly a future Astromg? You'd think that the French could spell correctly the name of the guy who has won the *Tour de France* the last three years, even if he is American: Lance "ARMSTRONG."

I still have a couple of copies of the paper.

***

Speaking of the rain, I have lived all my life in San Diego. That might not make sense to you right away, but I'll explain.

Here it has rained for more than a week without stopping. If it rained for more than a week in San Diego without stopping they would start talking about disasters on a biblical scale. People would run naked in the streets, never to believe in modern society again. Buildings would go up in flames, and the entire Y2K disaster would strike and wreak havoc on every form of life except some places in South America, Siberia, the South Pacific, and Africa.

But in *France* it merely puts a little damper on the bicycle training and morale.

Meanwhile, the sun has come back here, but I have to admit I was getting kind of worried.

***

Another subject. All of my work for the last two months will come down to Monday morning at 9:00 when I present my project.

My subject is "War and Film." I have taken the liberty of changing the subject to "War Films and the Changing Society, Through the Objective Eyes of Film-Makers."

I am going to explain the difference between two war histories written by Cornelius Ryan which were made into major films fifteen years apart. "The Longest Day," about June 6, 1944, and "A Bridge Too Far," about Operation Market Garden in Holland in the weeks just after D-Day, are the two book/films.

The first movie was made in 1962, while the latter was made in 1977. I am going to analyze the difference between the two eras to explain the glorification of heroism in "The Longest Day" and the anti-war feeling of "A Bridge Too Far."

I am very proud of all of my work and have learned a great deal about previous generations. I cover the assassinations of the Kennedys and Martin Luther King Jr. as well as the Watergate scandal, the Vietnam War and the Civil Rights Movement.

These events helped form the United States I come from, and even though for the moment I don't live there, when I get back I will look at my surroundings with new eyes. Many of the people I write to, like myself have not lived through this era, and I think it is crucial stuff.

It shapes who we are.

We all strive to know who we are, but some of us ignore the fact that you need to know who came before you before you can understand who you are at all.

***

On yet another subject, since it has been a while since I last wrote, I went to another AFS party, but it was the first party that I think my host-parents wouldn't have been thrilled that I went to.

First of all, the parents of the girl who threw the party left in the early afternoon. That's a major no-no. There was a lot of alcohol and a lot of really crappy food. That alone is nothing to get worried about.

Since this party was to celebrate all the birthdays that were in May for the people in AFS, with mine included, I was at party central.

Everybody walked around with a glass or even a whole bottle of something, and outside a lot of weed was being passed around. But I don't mess around with that kind of crap.

I went upstairs to get my camera, but little did I know that I was not destined to find it. I opened the door of my room, and there were two of my best friends playing the "Mommy and Daddy" game.

Throughout their *liaison* they must have had their door opened about ten times. I put a post-it note on the door that said *"occupé,"* but nobody saw it before opening the door.

Another friend of mine started making out with this girl. They hadn't known each other before that night. I was talking to people, but every once in a while I would look over, and they would be "over there" going at it, if you will.

Later, my friend came up to me and asked me what the name of his new girlfriend was. I told him what her name was, sure, but I came away so disgusted. I always viewed relationships more important than that.

The party turned into a complete hook-up party. Some girls came looking my way, but I'm not one to make such a foolish mistake. I don't think you can find somebody so amazing that you have to have them the first night. Most of the girls who talked to me were drunk off their heads anyway, so I pulled out my sleeping bag made an effort to doze off.

I have been to a lot of parties in *France*, but this one sucked. It wasn't all that fun, and then I had a headache the next morning.

The girlfriend relationships I've had have not been all that successful. Things would start quickly and end even faster. I got tired of all that bullshit. Because that's exactly what it is. B.S. Maybe I'm naïve and idealistic, but I always thought it should be better, more special than that. I don't want to get into a relationship only to see it die.

So it goes.

I don't know if this last subject was a good idea to write about, but I wanted to be honest and not hide anything. I have hidden enough about myself, and what I've come to figure out is it's not the best of ideas.

Malloire

***

One *peloton* training session on my bike, just like all the others that I do about five times a week, we started a climb that can go all the way to *Lamastre*, a picturesque town in the *Ardèche*, or we could veer off to *St. Félicien*.

Anyway, I was feeling particularly frisky, since it was a gorgeous morning and I had been riding like a king for the past couple days.

I went off the front and started hauling butt up and up and kept going on the route toward *Lamastre*.

I was having a great time and must have been about 500 meters ahead of the pack, out of site and around the bend.

I surveyed the view to my right. I looked down the mountain to the road below. I saw a group of cyclists calmly descending, swerving to and fro. It was majestic how they went from one side of the road to the other, always getting the turn right on the apex. It kind of looked like a snake slithering along. The jerseys were all nicely colored and -

"Oh Shit!" Those are my guys! My peleton had veered off to go to *St. Félicien*, not *Lamastre*, and left me to go on none the wiser.

I quickly turned around and started bombing down the hill. I was going 55 to 60 kph, working harder going downhill than I had going up.

I knew all these roads by heart and was using all my smarts to get around turns as fast as I could, only occasionally making sure that cars weren't coming. I didn't have to worry about cars from behind me since I was going faster than anybody in their right mind would go.

I made the turn and started up the climb to *St. Félicien* and finally caught a glimpse of the people who had slipped off the back of the main *peloton*. I charged by them. A couple tried to hop on to my wheel to see if they could follow me, but their hopes were short lived, I assure you.

I finally caught the leaders, who had stopped in a village at the top of the climb to fill their water bottles and wait for the slower people.

When I showed up they asked me where I'd gone and if I was feeling all right since I was so slow. I informed them of how hard I had been breathing to catch them up, and they seemed to understand.

I felt stupid, but it was all right since I had proved how strong I was feeling.

And it's a great story.

Chapter 20
Australian Chicks Rule!

5 juin 2002

Dear All,

I hope you are all doing well. I have done some cool stuff. Over my AFS weekend I really got a chance to escape from life a little bit. That's always a pleasure. We spent our nights in camping tents. We went canoeing down the *Chassezac* River. It was pretty calm but fun.

I did it with one of my best friends, an Australian named Emily. She's cool, so we founded the Australian/American canoe team. We tried to go faster than everybody else and to get through all the rapids faster than everybody else and had a great time doing it. It was awesome.

We partied every night, listening to music or playing the guitar. We slept in the same tent with another girl, but since the ground wasn't even, we had problems staying far enough away from each other to sleep well. We would all slide over to the lower side and bunch up there, practically on top of each other.

Sunday we went rock climbing. I didn't know how cool it would be. We climbed a stone wall (no indoor crap) from four different ropes in four different positions. I would climb up while Emily would be on the ground with the rope, making sure that if I did fall it wouldn't be too far. I did the same for her. But we climbed high up. I can't estimate too well, but it was at least 30 meters. It was scary.

I never fell, but it was complicated with normal tennis shoes. I felt like I did pretty well, as I do have a good power-to-weight ratio. If I had good handholds, I could let my legs go to try to find something to let me go even higher.

But to get back down is more complicated and much scarier. It was a trust issue with Emily, who was holding my rope, but I did not want to let go of that rock. That was my lifeline. Without the rock, I wasn't safe. But to get back down I had to let go of that rock and depend on my rope and Emily. I wasn't too happy about it. I was tense.

Once I finished climbing I would look around and say, "My goodness, how did I get so high?" When I was climbing all I saw was the rock, so I had no idea that I was somehow leaving the ground.

Obviously I did get back down, or I wouldn't be writing this to you.

Emily (right) with her friend Lea

And the whole weekend was unbelievably beautiful, but it was hotter than an oven. It must have been 40° C (105° F). We were baking. Anyway....

***

School is pretty much over for me. My project was very well received.

I have one hour of class left tomorrow and then on Friday everybody is going to get together for a picnic on school property to say goodbye to each other. There's no hiding it. I'm coming home soon.

I don't know what it will be like back home, which is pretty weird, considering you generally know what's going on at home.

All I know is that in a little less than three weeks I have the biggest race of my life, and my jersey number is 10744.

The *Ardéchoise* is the largest bike race in all of *Europe*, and it has been a goal during all of my stay in *Tournon*. Then after that I will have the biggest challenge of my life: *le Ventoux*.

I really need to train more, but the weather is sucky, and it doesn't stop raining. I have a running course, which obviously takes less time than being on the bike, but right now the path is muddy, and I need cycling kilometers on my legs anyways.

We'll see how it all works out. I'm looking forward to seeing all of you again.

Malloire

***

And thus concluded my letters.

Not this book though. The next part is directly meant for you. From this point on, I didn't have that much time. I was working against the clock. It was hard. I didn't write any more letters, but I still had a lot to say. So here goes.

Chapter 21
Le Dauphiné Libéré

11 juin 2002

Through my host-parents I got a VIP pass to a famous professional bicycle race called *le Dauphiné Libéré*. This year Stage 2 was starting in *Tournon*.

What was really exciting is that Lance Armstrong was in the race. What was even more exciting is that the stage went and finished on top of *le Mont Ventoux*. Lance Armstrong was leaving from my home town and finishing on top of the mountain I was determined to conquer.

What could be better?

All the team cars slowly started to arrive in the town center. Lance's team, US Postal, had an enormous trailer for its riders. Viatcheslav Ekimov (winner of the 2000 Olympics Time Trial in Sydney) came out. I shook hands with him and explained that I was from San Diego. He seemed very interested.

Actually that's a lie I tell myself to make myself feel better about myself, myself. He kind of brushed me off, but I didn't feel too bad about it.

Then everyone crowded around where Armstrong was supposedly going to come out.

We waited.

And waited.

And waited some more until he finally came out. I was close enough to touch him. I tried to give him a newspaper with his photo for him to sign, but other people got to him first.

He signed several autographs. Then he took mine and appeared about to begin writing . . . before deciding that four autographs was enough, and he didn't need to sign one for a kid who had only traveled over 9,000 kilometers, spent an entire year in a cycling country training to climb a mountain that he was going to conquer that very day and was an American in *France*, just like he was.

Of course, I didn't have time to explain all this to him, but that evening my disappointment was obvious to my host-family.

At least I got to take pictures of *Richard Virenque*, the most popular of all the French riders. He signed a cycling cap for me. I also got to shake hands with some of the best cyclists in the world.

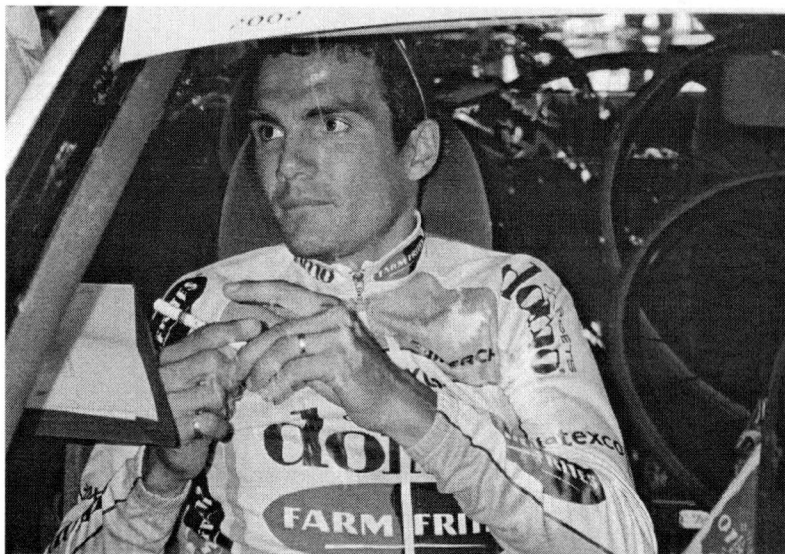

Richard Virenque in his team car

I had done so many cool things that day, but my goal of connecting with Lance was left unachieved. I went home and had a glass of wine and slept.

I felt understandably better afterwards.

Chapter 22
L'Ardéchoise

My American Dad came back over to France to see the biggest race of my life (so far) and introduce me to Susan Ten Eyck, his new significant other. I had heard a lot about her since I'd been talking to Dad on the phone about once a week.

I had to go meet her now.

I went to the *Valence* train station. There are two train stations in *Valence,* and I went to the one they told me they would be at. I waited, and waited, ran around to see if I had missed them, and finally sat down and wondered where the hell they could have been. It had been 30 minutes since their train was supposed to arrive.

I had a feeling, so I went to meet a small train that just arrived. Sure enough they were there and dealing with their huge baggage. I helped them out. They had arrived at the *Valence TGV* station on the outskirts and had to take a local train to the central station, which obviously took a little bit of time.

We went to rent a car, and while the rental car people were finding something for us we went into a local *bar* and watched the U.S. versus Germany World Cup soccer game.

It was a great game, a close game, but we lost.

I got to talk to Susie, which I greatly appreciated. She seemed very nice and very interested in what a seventeen-year-old bum had to say. She cared. It was nice.

We went straight to *Tournon,* to see *Lou-Lou* and *Jean-Claude.* They appreciated meeting Susan and seeing Dad, but the "travelers" were very tired and needed to hit the sack, so they soon went to their hotel and slept. We all needed to get up very early the next day to see my race.

I woke up at around five and had a pasta breakfast. *Le Ventoux* had already taught me that I have problems with exhaustion since I am so thin, so I have to eat a lot before and during something so long and hard as this race would prove to be. It's 120 kilometers of the most mountainous roads the *Ardeche* region has to offer.

I had a good breakfast. I was ready.

It was also hot as hell. It was barely light but already 30° C. This would prove to be a very interesting day by the time I got to the finish line.

I put my bike in the car. I thought I had everything ready, so we left. We got reasonably close to the start in *St. Felicien*, got the bike out, took some pictures, then I was off to the start.

I had a cell phone with me so I could call if I needed help or anything. They planned on meeting me after the first big climb in the same small town where I thought there was a wedding but there really was a funeral. The first climb today would be where I got hypothermia in February, when it started snowing.

So I had lots of fond memories.

Off I went, feeling like a million bucks doing my small warm up to get to the starting line.

HOLY SHIT! I forgot something. The little magnetic bracelet thingy you're supposed to wear around your ankle so that your time gets recorded automatically was far away. It was at home!

I was screwed. I had to go around and ask if it was something that I could get replaced. It wasn't, so I was in between a rock and a hard place.

I didn't have anyone holding my place in line after all, so I was not the first person to leave. In fact, I waited an hour and 40 minutes before I even got to the starting line. When I did get there I was really ready to kick some ass.

Some of my friends were at the starting line. They saw me as I was leaving, shouted out my name, and cheered. I smiled but kept on going. It was the last time I would see them.

I followed a very good experienced rider up the first climb. We must have passed 500 people. It was amazing. I felt great.

I was working hard as we climbed to the high village of *Nozières*, where Dad, Susie, *Jean-Claude* and *Lou-Lou* were waiting for me.

Nozières, visible in the saddle of the mountain. The grass is pointing at it.

In the town square in front of the church there is an old spring-fed fountain. I refilled my Gatorade bottles and shared a few war stories with everyone. There was lots of laughing. I was feeling great.

Susie, Lou-Lou, Jean-Claude et moi

Soon I was soon making the long descent to *Lamastre.*

That was one of the scariest parts of the day. People were all over the place. There was an ambulance every 400 meters and for good reason. There were too many people.

I didn't see any accidents, but a couple almost happened. I had the descent memorized, but I was petrified of all these people flying down this slope at 60 kilometers per hour without helmets on.

At the bottom there was immediately another uphill section. This one was shorter than the first, but still it was ten kilometers long.

At the top of this climb there was a rest stop, but way too many people were resting and drinking. It must have taken me five minutes to go 100 meters to get to the other side of this town.

Working on my farmer tan at 55 kph

Down a hill, and then up the biggest climb of the day. This climb was 16 kilometers long, and it hurt.

A friend of mine, also a strong cyclist, had seen me while I was going by so he sped up to say hi. He was a great deal bigger than me and should have been a lot faster, but I had already made up 40 minutes on him. He and I took turns drafting off one other, but as soon as the hill started to hurt I never saw him again. He dropped to the side and tried not to make it obvious that he couldn't stay with the American kid.

By this time it was really starting to get hot. It was around 35° C (95° F). I was starting to slow. I wasn't passing people with the same regularity as before. Up the rest of the hill in the heat, down in the heat, up a little hill I had never done before in the heat, then down a bit, in the heat.

The last climb is unbelievably challenging, even with fresh legs. It is 15% (incredibly steep) for just long enough that your legs threaten to stop working. Only willpower keeps them going.

By this time I couldn't see straight. It was now over 38° C, and I was out of gas. For the first time some people were passing me. I was in the hurt locker.

The last kilometers of the last climb were written on the ground with huge spray-painted numbers. I could barely see them through the tears that never seemed to move from my eyes.

I counted off the last five kilometers in my head as I passed over the painted numbers on the road. I finally got to the top. There was a rest stop but I knew that if I stopped I wouldn't get going again.

The descent came immediately after and would be a return to the bottom of first downhill of the day, which now we had to climb to get back to *St. Felicien*.

Ironic since there was such a contrast between how I was feeling at the end and at the beginning of the day, on the same mountain but going opposite directions.

I picked up speed downhill, and the wind wiped my tears away. I could finally see. It was a really fun descent. The road was closed so there were no worries of oncoming traffic. I swerved all over, throwing my bike and my body deep into the turns. The entire time going down I thought about the many long hours I had trained on this climb.

The last climb began. My mind wandered back to one particular morning when I stopped here to eat and noticed a French *Mirage* fighter jet heading right for me, skimming through the valley at several hundred kph. I waved as he burned right over me. He waved back with his wings, which wagged from side to side.

I thought about all this because I wanted the time to pass. I wanted to go home.

Around the last corner, and there was the sign *"Arrivée."*

I'm passing people again with 50 meters to go

Susie and Dad spotted me just as I reached the finish line. They rushed over, and we hugged.

On the way to the athletes' meal I realized how tired I was. Dad held me steady on my bike as I rolled along.

The town of *St. Felicien* was one big cycling carnival. Its population had increased ten- or twentyfold for the day. I set down my bike, ate a bit of the food, and then we made our way home.

I had done the 120 kilometers of climbing in a little under five hours, which was my goal. I was sick. I had gone too far. I wanted to throw up.

In the car we followed the winding *Ardèche* roads back down to *Tournon*. It was scary. I felt terrible. Susie was getting car-sick. It was so hot, and my head felt like it was going to cave in. It didn't, though.

I took a nap. Then we all got dressed up for the best meal I have ever eaten. We went to *"Chez Pic"* in nearby *Valence*, the most famous and expensive *restaurant* in the entire region.

I ate so much. It was a sort of thank you to my host-parents from Dad and Susie for helping me all year. My host-parents really cared for me to an extent you could not possibly expect. It was very special.

At the restaurant though, I had never eaten better. The meal did drag on a little and I was falling asleep since it was after eleven o'clock, and I had accomplished something very great that same day.

***

The next day Susie and Dad left. Had to get back to work in San Diego. They had come to *France* for the weekend just to see me. How 'bout that?

And Dad would be returning in just three week's time to climb with me *l'Alpe d'Huez* and *le Ventoux*. Oh yes!

***

The impending end of my time in *France* is a cause for personal reflection.

Often at the close of the day, I sit on the sill of the front window and look out at the sunset. I look out and realize that one day is ending, that another would soon be starting, and that I would have stuff to do.

Me and my windowsill

I sit quietly with my mouth closed, breathing through my nose, usually with my legs hurting from cycling, and I think of happenings all over the world.

I wonder what my friends in America are doing, and even my friends who aren't as far away as that. I hope they are as peaceful and happy as I am.

I have enough good will to share, if only that were possible. I am thankful that my time is coming to an end, and that it has been so long and so good.

The *Ardèche* from my windowsill

Chapter 23
Last Goodbye

16 juillet 2002

The last AFS reunion was not like the others. There was more spirit, more heart. It started with the *train grande vitesse*. That should have been an indication that this reunion wasn't like the others, but I didn't pick up on it as quickly as might have been convenient.

I was at the train station much earlier than the others because my host-parents had an appointment to get to and they wouldn't be able to drop me off afterwards.

So I waited around. I bought magazines. I read them. I bought a *sandwich*. I ate it.

And then a friend of mine showed up. She was an American, but we still talked in French. Her host-Mom and she were obviously very close so they had their panties in more of bunch than I did. When everybody else started to show up people started to cry, girls started to hug, couples started to make out, and I felt out of the loop.

I had nobody, I wasn't crying, and I certainly wasn't making out with anybody. People were crying because other people were crying.

I was waiting for my best friend, Emily. People surrounded me, but I had nobody to hang around with without Emily. I went around from group to group without finding my place, without feeling comfortable. Looking back now it was something I went to go look for in *France*, yet at the end of my stay, I was still looking for it.

Anyway, we got on the train. I was worried because I still hadn't seen Emily and we were already moving. I go and I find my seat. A girl from AFS sits down next to me and then her best friend takes my seat as soon as I offered it to her. This girl had just said goodbye to her host-parents, and she could not control her emotions and seemed to be drowning in her own tears.

I went to go find another group of AFSers and finally from one of the other cabins she arrives. What a relief! My Emily had arrived. Finally I had reinforcements. With Emily around I was able to find my place with the others.

The whole train ride to *Paris* on the *train grande vitesse* was full of music, laughter, and discussion. Everybody had a great time, but most of all everybody was nervous as hell. Nervous to go home. Nervous that they would find things had changed. Nervous that home wouldn't be home anymore.

Yet just about everybody was happy that his or her year of discovery had come to an end. Everybody felt a great sense of unity because everyone knew that they were going home. We were going home.

That was really hard to grasp. Home was a place that was safe, except we didn't feel comfortable going back to where we came from. We felt that we had learned so much here, and going back might undo that.

We felt threatened by home. It was a scary time.

When we arrived at the train station in *Paris* we unloaded all the baggage. I only had a backpack as I was going to meet up with Dad and go back to my host-family and then pack up.

But there were a ton of girls with much more baggage. It was almost impossible. I helped out these ladies because they would have been lost without me.

They could barely hold their small baggage, while dragged the big ones. This one girl must have had over 45 kilos of luggage all by herself. She didn't want to ship it, so she ended up dragging it.

I ended up shipping over 20 kilos of random things myself, so at least I didn't have to drag it.

I seriously felt sorry for her.

Even Emily was up to her eyes in baggage. I helped where I could, but these ladies were almost helpless. We went to a meeting point where other people from AFS were.

There was a very large demographic of people. From Americans to a nice guy from Ghana. I talked with lots of people, and as we got on the bus I struck up a nice conversation with two girls from the U.S. Only one of them was on the year program like I was, while the other girl was on the three-month stint.

They were very interesting but you could see that the girl who had stayed for only three months didn't feel as strongly as the other girl and I did, and we tried to compare what going home would be like. She felt that her life would kind of pick up where it left off, whereas my life had changed so much that I didn't know to where to pick up my new life from.

She was also hot. (I felt I needed to add that detail.)

We finally got to the hostel where we were staying, unloaded all the baggage, and settled into our rooms. Except for me.

I couldn't find the guy I was rooming with, so I didn't get to put my stuff down because he had the key.

I hooked up with all the people that I came to *France* with last September, and we reminisced about our troubles.

Everybody made an effort to meet everybody. We got our meal tickets and we ate. It wasn't all that good, but food served at these AFS functions was never good. At 8:00 we were supposed to be in this theater for a talent show. As I had no talent presentable, I didn't put my neck out, but others sure did.

Before the talent show a man who was heading things up for AFS came out to give us rules and other boring things he felt obligated to say.

He also took that opportunity to introduce everybody. He yelled out, "How many people here are from Europe?" Then there was a little cheer while they all stood up.

"Who's from South America?" The applause was louder as they took their turn standing up.

"Who's from Australia and New Zealand?" All the Australians stood up and cheered. They were a loud bunch.

"Who's from North America?" he continued. All the Americans and Canadians and Mexicans cheered.

What he said next was very special. We felt all as one. We were unified. "Now who's from Africa?" he asked.

There was a one-second silence as the two people from Ghana stood up. They stuck out of the crowd, as they were the only two black people.

Then everybody stood up applauding. It was loud, but that wasn't the point. We were there applauding their bravery and courage.

The goal of AFS is to understand and appreciate diversity. We had accomplished just that. It showed us that if we were supposed to accomplish one thing that year, we had done it. Our year had succeeded. We knew it was all worth it. Nobody in that room felt higher or lower than another. We felt enlightened.

Yet we also knew that it was all over. There were some tears, but those were just the first in a series to come that night.

***

The talent show got underway. The first act was a nice young American girl who played piano and sang. She was really amazing. She sang her heart out. I hadn't ever seen her before, but she was fabulous. When she finished everybody applauded long and hard.

There were some really good acts, like my German friend Sebastian who played the flute, and then he started to play two different sized and sounding flutes at the same time. It was really cool.

But then there were some stupid acts like the New Zealanders who did the cheer for the "All Blacks," the national rugby team. It was fun, but it didn't go along with the mood most people seemed to have.

Then a slightly chubby American girl went up to the piano, sat down, and played a very old song that turned out to be the perfect song to play.

She played John Lennon's "Imagine." It was amazing. Most people there spoke English fluently, even those with a background in Spanish.

And everybody knew this song. When the song would get a little complicated and not everybody would know the words we just rocked back and forth. Some people took their lighters out. A friend of mine who was sitting in front of me burned her thumb on her lighter.

That song turned out to be emotional for almost everybody. Americans were thinking of September 11th and home, while the others were sympathizing and thinking of their homes. Some came from Argentina, where the country was in turmoil. Others just thought of the world in general.

I didn't cry at any other point that whole weekend, but that was a special moment. We were about to say goodbye to our friends, and would probably never see them again. We were turning a page in our lives. The people that we had worked so hard to know would be leaving us for as long as we could foresee.

And that's what happened between Emily and me. We walked around together that night, but we knew that we would soon be on opposite sides of the world. And after this year in *France*, we knew how far that really was. It was a desperately sad night for me, so I tried to joke around as much as I could to hide it.

She went to bed after the Australians started drinking (which was strictly forbidden), and I'd gone to find my roommate just before. She ended up sleeping alone that night, so I probably should have stayed with her, but it didn't turn out that way.

I finally found my roommate, but he was drinking vodka in the room with a couple other guys, with me trying to sleep. They didn't sleep at all that night. I tried to, but I woke up at 5:30 and went and got a paper. I wasn't supposed to leave the supervision of AFS, but I figured they weren't awake anyway.

When Emily woke up, she had to leave. I still had another day there. I gave her a hug, helped her with her baggage, and then watched her go. I didn't know if I was ever to see her again, and I knew then that it was just a preview of what was in store for me.

***

I never really stressed how important my friends at school in *Tournon* were. They were the people I was in contact with all the time. I learned all my slang from them, and they taught me more than I could have ever imagined at the time.

I loved all of them, even when we had our differences. We showed *Tournon* our feelings about *Le Pen*. We ditched class and took the train down to Valence together. We got drunk during the World Cup when *France* was losing terribly.

We were great friends. They respected me for cycling better than any French kid, caring about speaking correctly, and being outgoing. They almost all smoked cigarettes and "other stuff," but I wasn't about to hold it against them since I was a visitor to their territory.

All of them learned to speak openly with me, even if we didn't speak a lot. Some of them waited around at the starting gates of the *Ardéchoise* for hours just to see me and shout my name when I went by. I can't imagine anything more caring.

This next picture is on the last day of school, where I am not ashamed to admit that I had had a little bit to drink and am holding up my report card with pride.

After recognizing all of the great friends I had, I think it's important to recognize the best teacher I've ever had.

M. Belliard was the most caring teacher I have ever known. He got down on our level and taught us World History like he was talking to us. He was pumped about what he was teaching. (He is reincarnated in my current history teacher, Mr. Greenstein, but let's not get sidetracked.)

My Class, me 3rd from right, front row, *M. Belliard* 2nd from right, 2nd row

Occasionally *M. Belliard* would come into class unshaved and unshowered, showing us that just because he was an adult didn't mean he was perfect or that it was easy for him to get up either. He made fun of me, insinuating that I took performance-enhancing drugs after I had made it into the paper for winning a race.

His class was the only one I ever studied for or worked at in any way. He is a great man. His class is the only one I passed, except for English. Strangely enough, he was the only teacher that I bothered to learn the name of. I hope one day he sees his name in this book. It'll make him smile to think that a slacker like me actually wrote something that wasn't in his class.

I just hope I spelled it right.

Getting back....

***

The rest of the AFS weekend in *Paris* wasn't really important. It was just one more day, and there was a bunch of crap we had to do.

We had to fill out forms on how AFS worked for us in our experience. That night was actually kind of cool. There was a party thrown by these Italian 12- to16-year-olds that we joined, so there was a lot of dancing, singing, and having fun. It was just a good time.

But I was thinking about Emily who had to be on a plane still and who would be on it for a good time longer. At that very moment he must have been passing by China before she got a connection to Melbourne.

When it was my turn to get on a bus, I got on with a friend named Maggie. She was going to the *Gare du Nord* to meet her Mom and grandmother under the *Departure* sign. I went to accompany her. I was going to make sure she got their just fine, and then I would take the subway to the airport to pick up my Dad.

I wasn't really in a rush to go pick him up.

Maggie did indeed meet with her Mom and grandmother. She had been rushing around, dodging in and out of people bigger than her, desperately trying to catch a glimpse of her Mom. She kept on walking but going as fast as if she was sprinting. She got next to her Mom and waited for her to turn around.

At once there was a reunification that I wasn't really ready for. These women were hugging and crying and mumbling incomprehensible things. I introduced myself once they calmed down. Her Mom was actually kind of funny saying, "Oh, well thanks." All she forgot to say at the end of the sentence was goodbye.

But I'm a bright guy, and I took the hint.

I said, "Oh yeah, I've got to get going, my Dad will get to the airport soon, and I don't know what the subway schedule is."

I added a quick "nice to meet you," and all of a sudden I was on my way. It was amazing. I finally was independent. Nobody was looking after me and there was nothing or nobody holding me back. I was at a high.

I went to go get a subway ticket. I got in line, and when I finally got to the front some guy cut in front of me. I said to myself, "I'm on a high cloud and I don't feel like knocking this guy off of his," even though he probably deserved it. I felt great.

And what's even better is that when I found the train I was supposed to get on I said to myself, "I'm thirsty." I walked by a soda machine and it already had *2 euros* in it. So I got a soda and I got *1 euro* back.

FREE MONEY! You couldn't possibly ruin my day. I had my head up high and was walking tall. I was in a country where I felt at home. I spoke like a real Frenchman.

I was the king of my own domain.

I was out standing in my field.

I got to where I was supposed to wait for Dad and set up camp. I even made a little sign like those guys who are supposed to pick up important people. I wrote "Mallory" on a piece of paper and just waited. I wasn't allowed to go into the actual terminal so I just had to wait around.

An hour later I was kind of getting worried.

I put away my sign and went to sit down. After a little bit of rest I got back up and waited in front of those doors where everybody was coming out except my Dad.

But then finally he poked his head out the door. He had no baggage. I'm thinking, "No, not again." He told me that he'd been waiting for a while and nothing had come out. I snuck in with him, a big *"faux pas,"* and as soon as I arrived the baggage came out.

Of course I took all the credit.

Soon we were on our way to the up *TGV* station to catch our train to *Lyon.*

We get on the first class coach because last time Dad had a bad experience with people smoking in a train car where there is absolutely no air circulation. First class is non-smoking, so it was worth the extra expense.

We get to *Lyon*, go to pick up the rental car, and guess who's there. It was Maggie and her parents. We both left from different Parisian train stations, but we arrived at practically the same time. I said one last goodbye, and soon Dad and I were on our way.

We get to my house and pick up what I've already packed to go on our little adventure in *les Alps*, with my two *Look* bikes in the car. We leave right away after saying goodbye to my host-Mom and passing on a hello to my host-Dad, who was working at the time.

Chapter 24
Mountain #1

19 juillet 2002

L'Alpe d'Huez was our first mountain to conquer.

After planning to climb it several times and having it not work out, I was a little frustrated and eager. We ended up staying in a hotel in *Vizille*, an *Alpine village* not far away from the bottom of the climb. The town was really small, and the hotel cost us just *26 euros*. And we ended up sleeping well.

Dad woke up before I did, but he woke me up so we could make it to breakfast. We made sure that we ate really well. I was wearing my cycling clothes so there were already some people looking at me a little sideways.

We finally got in the car and drove a little closer to one of the most famous cycling climbs in the world. It had been in the *Tour de France* many times before, but not this year, for better or worse.

In the village of *Bourg d'Oisans* at the bottom of the climb we got the bikes out of the car, and Dad went and got sandwiches, which was not easy to find at 10:00 in the morning. We put Powerbars and our camera in our pockets, and we were off to make history. Our own history.

I look at the picturesque *alpine village* we're leaving. It's beautiful, and everything's green. It's one of the most beautiful places in *France*. Then I look at the mountains on both sides of the valley. It looks like *Bourg d'Oisans* is at the bottom of a giant "V." *L'Alpe d'Huez* is at the top of one side of this picturesque valley.

Photo Credit: Breton Photo

Once you have zigzagged to the top of *l'Alpe d'Huez* there is no "other side" to go down. This magical road, the source of a country's pride, has no other purpose than to go up to a ski station.

What an engineering feat! Both sides of the valley look too steep for a mountain goat, let alone a road. 1,103 meters vertical rise in 13 kilometers of climbing. Several sections at 12%!

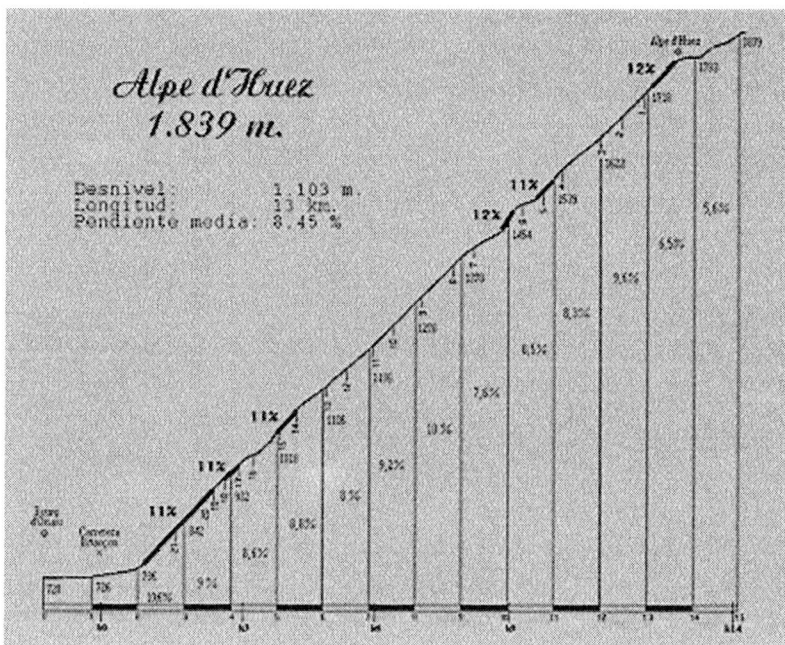

Photo Credit: easyweb.easynet.co.uk

We start the climb. I'm awestruck as I look up at what is in front of me. It's straight up!

I try to stay right by Dad as we begin, but he gets slower and slower. Finally we get to the first switchback. These hairpins are numbered, starting with number 21 and counting down as you climb to the top.

The first switchback honors Fausto Coppi, who won in 1952, the first time *l'Alpe d'Huez* was included in the *Tour de France*. Lance Armstrong's name is there, too, since he was the most recent person to win, which was just last year. Each switchback is dedicated to a different past winner.

As we passed this first of 21 signs, Dad's spirits were not too high. He had been training for this in San Diego since the fall, but that was almost impossible to do properly since climbing *l'Alpe d'Huez* is like climbing 13 kilometers of stairs, it's that steep.

Dad has been an athlete all his life, and now it seems like he's being made a fool by this climb. It's weird to see him falter at anything athletic. He's a national champion rower and has always been active, but this climb does not care about past accomplishments; it will try to defeat you every time you attempt it.

I can relate to this, since I have been forced to cower before several mountains, but this was not a day when I would be humbled.

I was feeling great along side Dad's agony. I was really strong. I hadn't been riding for a while because I wanted my legs to be "new and frisky." So when I actually arrived at the base of this climb I knew that I was going to feel well.

I was on a high, climbing up to the clouds.

I was feeling so strong that I actually pissed my Dad off. I was showing him that the road was so steep that if I accelerated quickly my front wheel would come off of the road and I could do a wheelie.

He wasn't amused. He said, "Philip, shut the fuck up." I did. I probably deserved that. It wasn't too sensitive.

After about six hairpins and going through a couple of towns we stopped and ate a little. Dad was complaining about how the gears on his bike might have been just fine for a climber like me, but they were too hard for someone at his level of ability, training, and age.

My speedometer showed I could just cruise at 12 kph and even shift up. At this speed my legs would turn the pedals at a comfortable cadence. The best poor Dad could manage in the lowest gear on my bike was 8 or 9 kph, and at that speed his legs were turning over painfully slowly.

While I was dancing on my pedals, he was doing heavy squats in the weight room.

And after a while he was down to 7 or 6 kph. The slower he went the harder it became.

Still he kept going, and he was surely not the slowest person on the climb that day.

Every so often someone would pass us going up. If he looked good I would accelerate and hop on to his wheel, maybe even take a turn at the front, leading him up the climb, before remembering my duties as a son and either waiting or turning around.

I had to prove to myself that I could match these other people, and each time I could, so it all worked out nicely for my ego.

Every once in a while we would look over our shoulders into the valley and see where we had come from. We could see cyclists crawling up the mountain, and we asked ourselves if someone had been looking at us with the same amazement.

I was working a lot less than Dad was on this climb. My legs were used to this after having spent a year climbing and training for *le Ventoux*, but Dad doesn't have a climber's body like I do, and he sure wasn't used to climbing roads at ten percent grade.

Plus, he's like, ancient. Forty years older than me!

The day was starting to heat up, and I was waiting for it to take its toll on me. I was wearing my *Ardèchoise* jersey and tights, looking good and still climbing with ease.

We stopped for a moment in a village 500 vertical meters below the ski station. I looked around. We were soooo high.

Dad was having trouble, but when we started up again he got an advance on me. I couldn't close it without using more energy than I wanted to so I just continued at my pace, and before I knew it I was on his wheel again.

He wasn't completely trashed!

We stopped a couple more times before getting up to the ski station, but I'll be the first to admit (and I won't feel bad about it either) that I was also hurting by the top. My lungs were gasping for air. My legs felt like spaghetti, but somehow we both kept going up.

I sped ahead to be able to get a picture of Dad going up. I got it, and I turned around to catch up to him. I kept on going, and then we were at the top.

Just like that.

We took some pictures, but I just wanted to get back down. It was incredibly pretty without the snow, though. The snow had made everything white, but now everything was a beautiful shade of green that you never get in San Diego.

You can look over to the other side of the valley and check out the mountains over there. It would be so peaceful to be a shepherd or something, cruising around up there, tending to your flock, looking around all day in the comforting shade of a thick tree.

I was pretty hungry and really looking forward to the descent. I put on a windbreaker, even though I really didn't need it, and down we went.

It was a really exciting descent, but not for the weak-at-heart. *Maman Lou-Lou* probably would have had a heart attack watching me go through those turns. We were hauling ass. It would have been scary to watch, and I sure wouldn't have wanted to race here.

The last hairpin turn we stopped and compared top speeds. Dad had gone 60.2 kilometers per hour and I'd only gone 60.0. I still had one straightaway left and I decided to go for it. I bombed that last 400 meters like my life depended on it. And when we got to comparing high speeds again I'd gone 61.2 kph. Victory!

Am I competitive or what?

We treated ourselves to an excellent pizza lunch in town somewhere. We kept looking back up to where we had been, and we walked a little taller after having conquered this mountain.

We had taken some great pictures looking down back to the valley floor. We had been somewhere else. We'd left Earth and gotten the chance to come back. Our surroundings were so unbelievably impressive. I had been there three times before to ski, but it was so much more rewarding to have made it to the ski station on my own power.

***

But what was coming next is what I'd been dreaming about since October.

Chapter 25
Le Ventoux

We headed south, out of *les Alps*, into the Mediterranean heat of Southern France. Headed for *le Ventoux*, the bald mountain, the giant of *Provence*, where my goals had been set for so long, at 1,912 meters. The toughest climb in *France*.

We arrived in the city of *Orange*, once a Roman fortress city, and not too far from our goal. Dad asked if that round, white outline in the distance was *le Ventoux*. I nodded quietly while saying to myself, "These dumb-ass goals of mine…how stupid can I get?"

Pretty stupid, let me tell you.

This is nothing like *l'Alpe d'Huez*, so recently conquered. Just like I remembered from my first trip to this mountain, the land is mostly flat, with vineyard after vineyard, and then you have *le Ventoux* looming over your shoulder, quietly observing. It's a scary prospect. Climb to the top of that?

Photo Credit: www.cotes-du-ventoux.com

***

We try to find a hotel in *Orange,* not an easy task with *the Tour de France* coming to town in just two days. We eventually do get a hotel, but it was the most expensive place in town, quite a contrast from the *26 euros* we spent the night before. We lay down for that night, and the next morning we slept in.

We did some sightseeing, including a very cool Roman theater still in use for concerts and plays. It was really a blast, but it was as hot as that place where the little guy with the pointy tail lives.

When we got to the top of the theater, to the nosebleed seats, we could look out to see where we would be climbing to the next day.

Daunting is all I had to say. You couldn't really escape it.

Waking up the next morning was not hard to do. I was pretty stoked. Dad and I made sure to eat as much as we could. We got everything in the car and drove off.

Photo Credit: www.lemontventoux.net

We drove 50 kilometers to the town of *Malaucène* at the foot the mountain. You could actually climb one side of *le Ventoux* from there, but I had no interest in doing that because the *Tour de France* wouldn't be climbing that side this year.

So Dad and I rode easily around the base of *le Ventoux*, chatting for 12 kilometers to the village of *Bédoin*, through which I had passed just months before on my first attempt at *le Ventoux*.

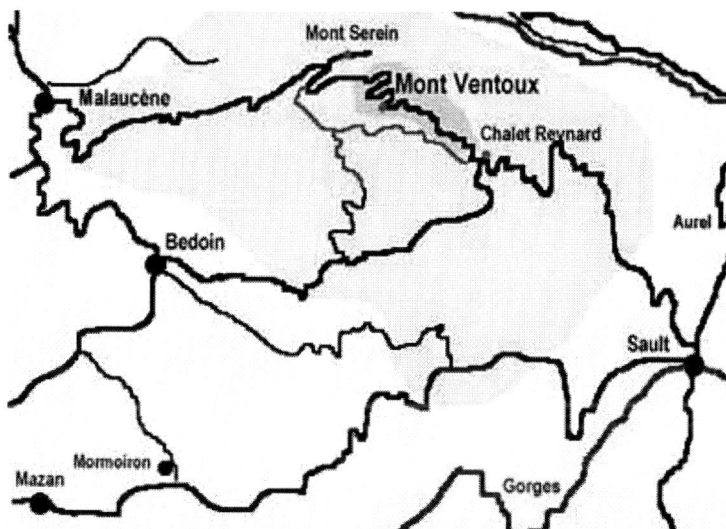

Photo Credit: www.geocities.com

The next day *Le Tour* would be passing through *Bédoin* on its way up to finish at the summit. We were now on the same roads that Lance was about to ride. I could feel the shot of adrenaline in my body.

I remembered that the road out of *Bédoin* starts at three or four percent, pretty mild, but then it spikes up to nearly ten percent four kilometers later. It's pretty amazing. You're going along just fine, and then you go around this hairpin turn, and you've got to be ready to shift to your easiest gear because you're going to need it badly.

It begins just like the climb to *l'Alpe d'Huez*, but unlike that climb, *le Ventoux* never slows down. It goes up and never,

155

ever levels out. On *l'Alpe d'Huez*, whenever you go through a village or just right after a hairpin turn, it levels out a bit so that you have the opportunity to breathe and give your legs a break. With *le Ventoux* there are no towns, no landmarks, just endless forest, and it never lets up.

And it goes up like that for over 17 kilometers. There's 50% more vertical rise than *l'Alpe d'Huez*. The Giant of *Provence!*

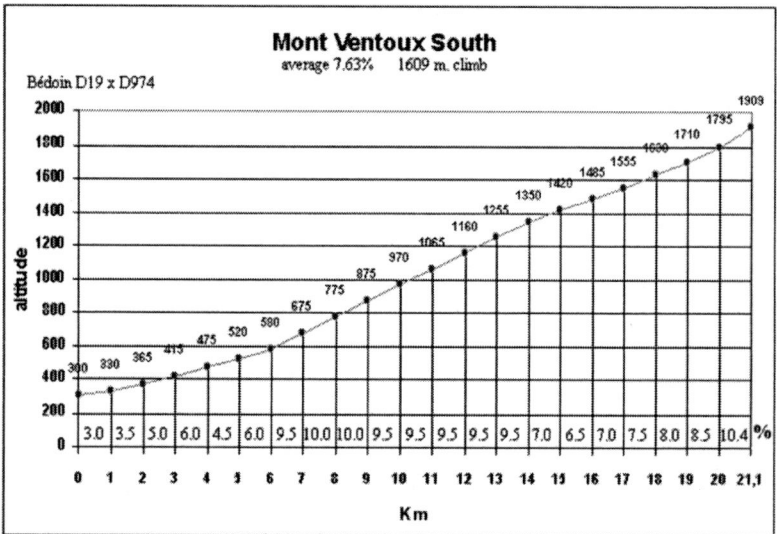

Mont Ventoux South
average 7.63%   1609 m. climb

Bédoin D19 x D974

Photo Credit: www.lemontventoux.net

This is what *le Ventoux* looks like statistically. It's a relentless climb, and when I finally get to the top, it will be a great feat. You might think that eight or nine or ten percent doesn't sound like a lot. I welcome you to catch a plane to *France* and go see *le Ventoux* yourself, because it is truly intimidating. Pictures can't do it justice.

Dad was looking and feeling better than at *l'Alpe d'Huez*, but it was much warmer than what he was used to in San Diego, perhaps 35° C at the bottom, and he was already dripping with sweat.

We made sure to eat well this time, and we were drinking all that we could. I was going to go leave this country in a few days, and if I left without conquering this beast, I would go home kicking and screaming.

I wouldn't be happy about it.

I think about all this as we approach *Bédoin*.

Dad on the road to *Bédoin*

The village of *Bédoin* was bustling with cars and motor homes and cyclists as we arrived. We joined in the steady flow toward the mountain.

Four kilometers outside of town, as we made that turn and started the real climb, I kept Dad right in front of me, making sure he didn't falter.

All the while, this trip was much more interesting than my last failure. This time I was no longer alone. I had Dad, and there were tens of thousands of people on the climb, in motor homes, on other bikes, in cars, tents, anything conceivable.

Tons of people were riding up the mountain, and Dad was holding his own.

I happened to be wearing my souvenir *Tour de France* polka-dot jersey. The person who wears that jersey is the points leader in the "King of the Mountains" competition. Whenever you pass over a mountain you get points according to your position. The guy with the most points wears this jersey.

At that moment a few hundred kilometers away, a Frenchman named *Laurent Jalabert* was wearing this jersey in the real competition, so I got a lot of encouragement from the thousands of people sitting on the side of the road, waiting patiently for the race to come the next day.

"Allez, JaJa!"

Once when I was actually in front of my Dad, who by the way ironically was wearing the souvenir white jersey of the best placed rider under 25-years-old in the race, somebody asked me in French, "What is *Jalabert* doing going so slowly up this climb."

I replied in French, "He's waiting for his old man." I gave a nod with my head that the old guy suffering behind me was my Dad. He acknowledged this but said, "Well, don't forget to win the race."

I smiled and kept on going.

But oh my, this was getting hard. On and on we climbed through the forest. I was concentrating on Dad so much I missed the marker where I had stopped last Spring.

***

Photo Credit: www.lemontventoux.net

By the last four kilometers we had emerged from the pine forest to find ourselves one-on-one with the sun. There were no more trees, only white rocks. It's barren, lifeless and windy. Everything is so bright that you want to keep your eyes closed and will yourself up the road.

You could see that the weather station really wasn't that far away anymore. Then, after a while, you don't see it getting any closer and realize that it really is going to be trouble getting there.

I stopped at the *Chalet Reynard*, the only structure on the whole climb, to get some water for Dad while he kept going.

I filled our bottles and busted my butt to get back. After about a minute of total suffering I got back to him. I handed him the water bottles, and I dropped back in agony.

After catching my breath I caught back up pretty easily, but by this point Dad was dying. He was going so slowly that I thought he might not make it to the top.

Photo Credit: www.lemontventoux.net

We had three kilometers to go, and we might have been able to walk faster. We were going unbearably slow. My legs were still working, but I wouldn't have been able to tell you so. Mentally I was in a ditch by the side of the road. I was a dead-man cycling.

We stopped every kilometer or so now and drank and ate. Dad struck up a conversation in German with a nice older guy. Then when we got going again Dad said we absolutely had to beat the German guy to the top. Guess Dad's as competitive as I am.

We didn't stop at the monument where Tom Simpson died. It was kind of spooky, how he died and about then how we wanted to.

Dad stayed on my wheel until we got to the very last corner that I had told him about all year: the mound where it spikes up to 20% for the last 25 meters before you hit the top.

I stand up on the pedals and sprint up the hardest part of the hardest thing I had done in my life, all the while with Dad right behind yelling, "Hurry up! You're in my way! Don't stop!"

I had to reply, "I *AM* going."

I really was. After all we had been through the old bastard wanted to go faster. HAH! Probably just saving face.

He had dragged himself up the mountain for so long, and then finally as the finish was only meters away he found the legs he needed for one final push over the top. His training did indeed count for something.

Bravo, Dad.

Chapter 26
Puke

We did it. We were able to look down all around us. There was no more up. Only down.

It was a beautiful moment, but I was tired. We bought some drinks and souvenirs at the store attached to the weather station, got this guy to take our picture, and then we went down the other side of the mountain straight back to the village where we had parked a little over four and one-half hours earlier.

The descent was a lot scarier than *l'Alpe d'Huez*. And what was worse, there were a lot of cars going down, too. I managed to weave through the traffic, but I was scared. I look at the odometer on my bike and it basically said to me, "Slow down, stupid."

I didn't. I kept going right on down.

I passed a sign that yelled, *"Caution, 12 pourcent grade."* I kept going down. I look at my odometer again. It said 75 kph, and it was climbing.

Then I see a sign that warned of a hairpin turn in 400 meters. I take that as my opportunity to slow down, but not before going an extraordinary 82.5 kilometers per hour.

Luckily I made the turn, and Dad followed, but he wasn't as brave (foolish?) as I was. Since I had my camera in my pocket I decided to pour on the juice and get far enough ahead of Dad so that I could turn around and take a picture.

That's not easy, as I figured out the hard way. I would get to where I thought I was far enough ahead, dismount, pull out the camera and turn around, only to see him whip by.

I'd then have to get back on my bike and try to get ahead of him again to see if I could pull it off the next time.

I did end up getting one good photo of him. Since there was 23 kilometers of descent I got to try several times.

As we very quickly dropped back to lower altitude it became hotter, and hotter, until you could have cooked an egg on the road if you had wanted.

We got back to the car, but the heat was absolutely suffocating. It was terrible. We had set off early enough so that the heat was manageable at the bottom of the mountain, and then as we climbed, the altitude had kept us at least relatively cool.

I puked half way home, but I wasn't going to let that ruin my experience. Actually I'm kind of proud of it now.

We scurried back to the hotel, very proud and very, very tired men. We ate well. It had been an amazing day, but I was in a hurry to end it. I quickly fell asleep, and we slept long and hard.

Dad and I woke up early, ate ravenously, and then we were on our way back to *le Ventoux*, this time to see the *Tour de France* go by. Lance Armstrong was in the overall race lead, and everybody was rooting for him.

As we were both very tired and we didn't want to go through the same experience as the day before, we decided to only go a couple hundred meters past where it started to get steep.

Little did we know how unbelievably boring the day was going to be.

***

We got there four hours before the riders were supposed to go by. And it was hot. It was hotter than hell. It was hot and dry and sweaty, just all around miserable. I sure wouldn't have liked to have been riding in the tour that day. It reminded me of what I read about Tom Simpson. He died on a day like this day.

Dad and I put some newspaper down in the shade and we actually tried to catch a nap. I slept a little, and I think Dad did, too, but it wasn't very satisfying.

We were looking forward to seeing the publicity caravan that comes an hour before the riders do. They toss out prizes and other stupid things, and I wanted them. I wanted to get to the side of the road and try to get my hands on some crap.

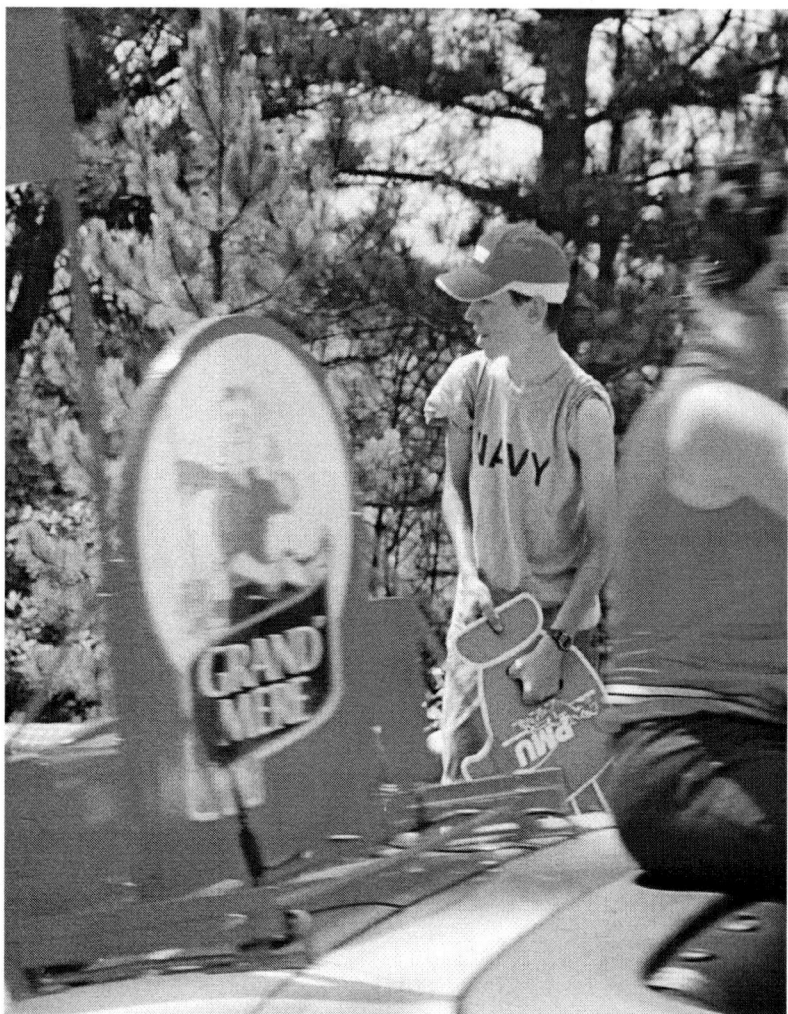

I fared pretty well. I scored one of those enormous green hands that you can see on TV, some gummy bears, a hat, a sausage, some cheese and coupons to a *supermarché*, along with other stuff I've forgotten about by now. The people in the cars would just toss the stuff out the window, and you'd have to grab for it.

***

But now that the publicity caravan had passed, everyone was anxious to see the riders. We looked for the helicopters that follow the riders to broadcast TV pictures from the air. We did finally see them, and they approached ever so slowly. Then as they got really close we saw cars passing us on the road again. They were what preceded the riders. There were team cars, officials, and VIP's. Then there was a gap. And then we saw motorcycles with TV cameramen sitting backwards on them.

And then the breakaway came into view. Eleven riders passed, including my old friend *Richard Virenque*, whose picture I had taken the month before at the *Dauphiné Libéré.*

They weren't going all that fast. People had been going up that mountain all day, and some had actually been faster than that. Except, of course, these professionals had been doing this for two weeks, and that very day had already been on their bikes for 190 kilometers. So we did feel a little sorry for them.

I snapped off some pictures, but I was waiting for my idol, Lance Armstrong. He's somebody I genuinely respect. He trains every day and has more commitment and drive than I could possibly imagine.

And he was coming my way. I saw him before the start of that stage of the *Dauphiné Libéré*, but I hadn't ever seen him in action.

***

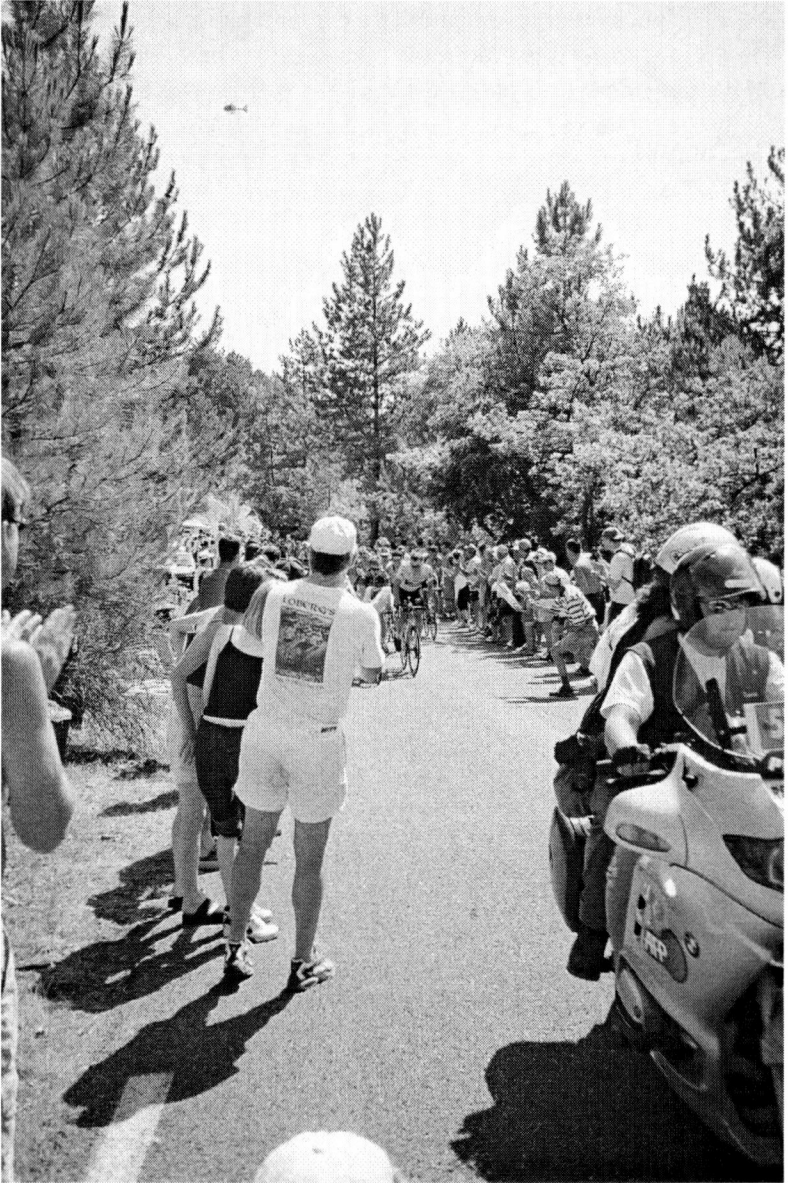

Helicopter above, Dad watching, Lance coming

I did see him, but I mostly saw him through the lens of a camera. And I have the proof. I have the pictures. I have many pictures of many people that I've seen on the TV so many times, and now I was close enough to touch them. It was amazing.

Lance came by much faster than the escape group, and he was calmly talking to a teammate while going up a road with a 10% slope. He looked great. He passed us, and already riders were streaming off the back of the *peloton*.

I took pictures of the most important people. We waited until everybody passed, and then we got back on our bikes to ride back down.

It was very weird. We'd been there for over four hours and watched them go by for 45 seconds. It was insane, much too much work, but somehow worth it now that I can look back at it. I can say I did it.

Anyway, we knew that if we didn't get the heck out of there right away the traffic would be horrendous. Getting down was a scary operation. Thousands and thousands of people were coming down that mountain. Most of them were walking, but we were riding. When we got back to the little village of *Bédoin*, there was a TV in the bar on the main square. The whole road was blocked with people watching that TV showing *Virenque* approaching the summit with Lance in hot pursuit.

Photo Credit: www.lemontventoux.net
Dad stopped a moment to watch while I kept going.

I get to the car first. Dad was pretty sore from the day before, so I ran behind and pushed him the last 50 meters. We got in the car and turned the radio on to see if we could hear what was happening on the mountain. Apparently *Richard Virenque* was still in the lead, but Lance was catching him up, and quickly.

We started driving back to *Tournon*. Apparently the mountain wasn't quite long enough for Armstrong, as he didn't quite catch *Virenque* for the stage win, but *Virenque* had been no threat to Lance overall. He was way behind in the general classification, since he had lost a lot of time in previous stages.

By coming in second on this stage Lance had made serious time gains against his true rivals to win *le Tour*, and it now looked certain that he would win overall.

*****

As Dad and I were driving in the car one of the funniest things of the whole year happened. The French radio was talking to the American comedian Robin Williams, who is well known in Europe and speaks decent French. He's a fan of *le Tour* and a great friend of Lance's.

They asked him how Lance would feel about the stage result. He said that Lance would be happy that his competition finished so far behind him.

Then they asked Robin what he thought about *le Ventoux*. He said that it was really amazing, and that on TV it couldn't show just how steep it was.

He continued in French, "It looks like a big . . ." then switching to English, he asked, "How do you say tit?"

The French announcer translated for him. He then said, "Yeah, it looks like a big tit, and the top is a big nipple."

Dad and I could barely look at the road we were laughing so hard. It was funny because we had never actually realized how much *le Mont Ventoux* really DOES look like a tit as it looms above the plains of *Provence.*

After we got over Robin Williams, we kept on going. We barely ran into any traffic. We had done a good job of getting out of there before the crowd. We got back home to *Tournon* around 7:30 PM, much to the surprise of my host-Dad.

We ate, talked and hit the sack. We were pretty exhausted.

Chapter 27
Finis, Enfin!

The next day was our day to pack everything, relax, say goodbye to my French family, and stumble around. Or maybe that was just my job. I was leaving everything I had learned to love. It was again very scary.

Une seule partie de ma famille francaise

We got our bikes packed, and all my clothes just seemed to barely fit in everything we had.

I kind of drifted through the whole day. We ate dinner, and Dad immediately went to bed. We were going to have to get up at five o'clock to be able to drive to *Lyon* in time to catch a plane to *Paris* in time to catch a plane to Los Angeles.

But I decided to stay up and watch TV.

I watched the first two episodes of "Band of Brothers," the American TV series that I was so ticked that I didn't see before I left. They were the episodes I had already seen, directly from the book that I had already read. When I eventually did go to bed it was just a little before midnight. I wanted to be good and tired when I got on the plane so that I might be able to catch a little bit of sleep. (It didn't work.)

***

Everybody got up at five, even my host-parents. They were looking sad. I couldn't blame them. They were letting go of something. I wasn't exactly doing the same. I was letting go of something to embrace something else. They were simply losing me.

Maman Lou-Lou was doing pretty badly. She was saying stuff like, "Take good care of yourself, you hear?" all the while crying. She wasn't doing a very good job of holding back the tears.

I said goodbye and walked out to the car.

I felt bad that I didn't feel bad.

That might sound a little weird but I felt guilty that I didn't cry and hug and feel really badly. I went outside, got in the car with my Dad and left. It was as simple as that. We got to *Lyon*, got on a plane, got to *Paris*, got on another one, and left the country that had been my home for a year.

***

We flew over Greenland. It was a clear day so I could see everything from the window. It was the iciest most barren place I'd ever seen. I guess that's why they named it Greenland.

In Los Angeles when we were going through customs we were standing in a long line with our carts packed to the brim with suitcases and bicycles and lots of other stuff. A Chinese gentleman cut in front of us, obviously not knowing what he was doing. Dad goes up to him and tells him to get into the back of the line like people do in "this country."

I learned a valuable lesson there. Sometimes it's not worth it. Pissing people off doesn't help anybody. It has to be done in certain occasions, but you've got to pick and choose your battles.

***

Then we were greeted by the new contingent of my family, namely Susan and her daughter Emily, with whom I had been in contact for a while over the phone and e-mail.

I don't know if I've ever been welcomed with such warmth. I realized finally that I was home, a place that I seemed to drag behind me wherever I went. I was there.

I didn't bring it there; it was put in front of me.

Conclusion

I came to *France* without expectations. But at the end I came, I saw, I conquered. The mountain that I conquered was fabulous. I felt that I had accomplished something great by getting to the top and that somehow it had summed up the year.

I know that it wouldn't have been nearly as special if I had achieved this feat at the beginning of the year. At the summit I knew that it was finally time to go home, that I was ready, that I could leave this country with my head high.

I had achieved so much, and standing at 1,909 meters was a symbol of my accomplishment.

Yet at the same time I feel that what I accomplished in *France* is only a chapter in the story of what my life will become. I'll have many more adventures, maybe even some worth telling. There might be a good story or two. They might even be fun to talk about, but I feel that I am destined for more.

How much more? I really couldn't tell you but, if I'm confident of one thing it is this: I'll have one hell of a time doing it.

Whether I write about it or not will not depend on how interesting it is. It will depend on the people I meet and how I change.

The people I met in *France* were very special to me, leaving me with a lasting effect, something I didn't really feel the depth of until I had been back home for over five months. It just goes to prove that you don't know what you have until you lose it.

As I write this I think about how lucky I am. I encourage

you to do the same. I am not talking about your financial status but the people you've met and how they change you and how you change them.

Tell the ones close to you that you love them and that you feel lucky to know them. Be a friend to everybody. Learn. Achieve.

Smile.

Epilogue

Since getting back and settling down I've had a lot going on.

We are a true family now. Dad and Susie have married, and I was the best man. Susie and Emily are almost the best influences I've ever had. Susie had big shoes to fill to replace *Maman Lou-Lou*. She has met the challenge most admirably, but Susie says she will never "replace" *Lou-Lou*, only carry on her efforts.

The two of them still talk on the phone, so you can be sure I am well taken care of.

Susie and *Lou-Lou*
***

We have cats and dogs, a lot like it was in France, and I have new aunts and uncles and grandparents. That's turned out cool.

Emily has turned into someone to whom I can completely open up. She knows all my secrets…almost.

As soon as I got home I had a chest operation at UCLA Medical Center. It's hard to explain what they were doing, but they were basically rearranging the "furniture." I have fully recovered now.

***

When I was in France the school curriculum was so rigid I couldn't really transfer any credits home, nor did I intend to, so basically I had a year off to learn French and ride my bike. Oh, yes! When I got home I had to repeat junior year of high school, so this past year I got to see all my Torrey Pines classmates during freshman and sophomore years graduate while I was "stuck" with the "young'ns," but I have been able to make some great new friends.

Throughout the year I was gone, one friend I frequently wrote to was Mallory. She was someone I met in P.E. before I left, and we quickly became friends because of the coincidence of our names. She was a freshman, while I was a sophomore, but after my year away we ended up in the same grade.

There were some things I needed to write down on some nights I spent alone and wasn't exactly comfortable putting them in weekly e-mails to the adults in my life.

She was really the only friend I had that spoke English. I was very proficient in French, but sometimes I needed to put my thoughts down in English. Just writing them is somewhat self-medicating for me, and knowing that someone was reading it was comforting.

Even though she didn't write me as often as I wrote her (She's incredibly busy, and I busied myself writing.), I enjoyed having her company 9,000 km away. After I returned we did not develope into the good friends I had envisioned, but we still talk occasionally.

I encourage you to be there for your friends as I try to be for mine because sooner or later they will need your shoulder.

***

I haven't cycled much this year, but I've rowed with Dad and Emily, and now I'm running and doing push-ups and sit-ups since I'm applying to ROTC programs and to the Naval Academy. I'll run in my first marathon in a few months.

***

The very day I left France Jean-Claude had a major heart problem. I don't exactly know what happened, but it was pretty scary. I feel guilty that my leaving might have contributed somehow, but I am proud that we were such a close family in France.

JC has had to retire, and he takes lots of medications and has to take walks around town.

***

We were reunited when Jean Claude and Maman Lou-Lou came to visit us in California in June 2003. We had a blast.

You can never have too many parents!

I hope to get back to see them in France many times in the years to come. We still talk over the phone regularly.

Family forever.

And I am the happiest I have ever been. I left for France because I was unhappy, and I returned with happiness in my pocket. I don't really know how it all worked out, but all the stories in this book are pieces to the puzzle of my present state. It was kind of a shock to come home. All the rules were different again, and I had to adjust, but after a couple of tumultuous months with my hard-ass Dad, I have emerged a complete person.

***

I have written this book to share all of my experiences with you, so that maybe you could learn the lessons I did without having to do what I did, climb a mythical mountain, because it was long and inconvenient and sometimes painful, and many of you don't have the time or the means to do what I did, but I definitely can say that I had the time of my life.

Check out the size of that sentence!